FALLING FOR HER RESCUER

BROTHERHOOD PROTECTORS WORLD

CHRISTINE GLOVER

Twisted Page Press LLC

BROTHERHOOD PROTECTORS

ORIGINAL SERIES BY ELLE JAMES

Brotherhood Protectors Series

Montana SEAL (#1)

Bride Protector SEAL (#2)

Montana D-Force (#3)

Cowboy D-Force (#4)

Montana Ranger (#5)

Montana Dog Soldier (#6)

Montana SEAL Daddy (#7)

Montana Ranger's Wedding Vow (#8)

Montana SEAL Undercover Daddy (#9)

Cape Cod SEAL Rescue (#10)

Montana SEAL Friendly Fire (#11)

Montana SEAL's Mail-Order Bride (#12)

SEAL Justice (#13)

Ranger Creed (#14)

Delta Force Strong (#15)

Montana Rescue (Sleeper SEAL)

Hot SEAL Salty Dog (SEALs in Paradise)

Hot SEAL Hawaiian Nights (SEALs in Paradise)

Dedicated to all the people serving this nation. Thank you for giving me a safe place to write all my words.

CHAPTER 1

JONAH LAWSON WRAPPED his headscarf around the bottom half of his face, covering his nose, most of his cheeks, his mouth and chin. The beard he'd grown and dyed dark brown before infiltrating El Muhunnad's terror cell itched beneath the rough, dirty fabric. And the brown contacts he'd been wearing since he went undercover stung his corneas as wind whipped sand and dirt against his face.

No one in his family would recognize him if they saw him today, not even his twin brother, Jacob.

Jonah swiped his eyes with a corner of his shemag, the traditional Afghanistan headscarf he'd been wearing for weeks while living in the cell's compound, then hefted his Soviet issue AK rifle. He scoped the terrain in the distance, watching for enemy encroachments. So far, he'd been lucky and hadn't had to shoot any American soldiers while assigned to this post.

Last thing he wanted was to blow his cover after busting his ass for months to gain the group's trust. They believed his backstory despite having his face having western features. That he'd betrayed his country after losing a woman he loved because of a fuck up with her commanding officer which the bastard covered up. The loss was real. The reasons behind the loss had been faked. But nothing he did could make them think he had faked his grief. No, he still blamed himself for her death. For failing to protect her.

He had to get them to allow him to do more than sentry grunt work. They'd bought his story about his father being an Afghan and his fanaticism growing year by year while he lived in the United States with his widowed mother. He'd painted himself as a traitor by giving them intel about the country they wanted to attack. Credible false intel which had opened the first doors into the cell.

Now he needed to get taken on a mission to discover their elusive leader and stop him from attacking yet another western target. In truth, he'd volunteered for this mission after losing his girl-friend Sandy to enemy fire which had downed her Blackhawk helicopter. She'd been hitching a ride to catch a flight to Stuttgart, Germany for a week of R and R.

But a missile had taken dawn the Army Lieutenant's chopper before she reached the base. He never wanted to go through that hell again. Next time he committed, he'd choose someone outside of the military. A civilian he could count on whose life he wouldn't have to worry about every day.

His eyes stung. Had to be grit. He rubbed them and concentrated on the road that led to the compound.

Jonah wanted to put these jackasses out of business. Permanently. But he'd have to practice a helluva lot of patience first. If he didn't cut the head off the snake, a new group would merely band together again under their wealthy, anonymous commander. Then they'd hide more efficiently and continue their war on everything he served to protect when he'd become a Navy SEAL.

He continued scanning for trouble until he spotted one of the compound's black Toyota Helix's kicking up dust and rocks in the distance. The truck climbed the winding mountain road, skirting the dangerous precipice while moving closer to the hidden terror cell's compound wall.

He looked through his scope and counted the occupants. Five. Four had left the terrorist's compound on a fact finding expedition in Kabul. Looked like they found more than a few facts. They found a woman. And from where he sat, he could tell she'd been roughed up a lot. Bruised cheeks and a split lip marred an otherwise perfect face.

Perfect and... a flush of adrenaline traveled through his veins. The pulse point in his temples punched his skull. Did he know her? What the fuck? Impossible. No way this could be Sandy. He'd identified the body and been a pallbearer at her funeral. But he thought recognized this other woman.

No way. He shook off the weird vibe and concentrated on figuring out how to rescue her. If she needed rescuing. He'd didn't want to scuttle this covert assignment to save her ass if not. Still, regret filled his heart. No way would she survive interrogation and far, far worse.

The truck motor echoed against the mountainside and reverberated into the still night air as it finished approaching the compound and barreled through the metal gate.

Stay put. Wait for orders. He looked at the truck below him as more wind and dust and sand kicked up into the air. Men shouting in Arabic several feet below him—the popular Dari lingo he'd had to become fluent in to infiltrate this group—reinforced his gut instincts about their plans for their captive.

"Get that bitch to the holding cell," his senior in command yelled. "And post double the guards. She's slippery as fuck."

Jonah's jaw ached. Every muscle in his body coiled, ready to spring into action. He channeled the adrenaline pumping through his veins into considering all the entry and exit points to the compound, eliminating the most obvious ones to the other men living there.

A slap, then the thud of a fist hitting flesh, echoed in the still night air followed by a high-pitched cry of pain. Shit. He'd heard and seen them beat others—all men... had even participated as part of his covert mission. But women? This was a first. Fuck. Now he'd have to compromise his mission.

The image of his girlfriend smiling just before she entered the Blackhawk helicopter to hitch a quick ride back to the main base flashed. They had never recovered Sandy's body. He'd be damned if he let this woman die too.

He heard the terrorists' captive scream. Glancing down, he saw them beating her again. His fingers itched, tingled as he gripped the rifle, fighting the desire to shoot to kill them all.

He couldn't risk putting her in the line of fire... nor would he jeopardize losing the chance to relay the intel he'd gathered.

More shouting... his alias name in the mix. *Show time.* He slid off the compound's top ledge until he stood on the one below. "What's up?" he asked in Dari, speaking to his roommate Azzam on the ground below. Not able to see where they'd taken their prisoner.

Azzam shifted his AK. "Get to the holding block,"

he said. "El Abid wants you to guard the prisoner we brought in."

Jonah didn't question the order. Simply nodded, then made his way down the ladder and jumped off. Moments later he arrived in the dank, musty corridor leading to the row of cells.

The scent of mildew mingled with urine and sweat as he made his way through narrow rows of cells. Overhead, ceiling lights encased in cages illuminated the cement walls and floors. Shadows warred with the pale glow reaching the prison door bars he passed until he finally arrived at the one holding their newest captive.

"Who is she?" he asked, skimming his fingers over the cold metal handle, his voice echoing off the thick stone walls despite his quiet undertone.

"Israeli scum." The man spit and the gob landed onto the metal door. "She's been playing us for fools for months, but no more."

Tension coiled inside his gut, rattling and threatening to strike the back of his throat. Was she Mossad or part of the Israeli Defense Force? Or something else? Another enemy disguised as a potential ally? "Good. One more infidel to kill." Jonah clapped the guard on his shoulder, feigning allegiance and happiness while the venom snapped against his breastbone.

"She's passed out. Shouldn't be a problem for

several hours," Azzam said. "Time enough for me to grab something to eat. You want something?"

"No." Even the idea of putting food in his belly brought bile into his throat. Jonah tilted his head toward the small window in the door to look at the woman who lay curled in the fetal position in the urine-soaked room's back corner. "I'll check her out. Make sure she's not dead. Wouldn't want to lose her intel before we finish her off."

The guard laughed. "Excellent idea," he said, then left Jonah standing alone by the prison cell's door.

As soon as the coast was clear, Jonah lifted the ring of keys from the metal spike on the opposite wall. He'd have to move fast, or he'd get caught and thrown into one of the other cells without a second thought. He stepped into the cell, then crossed the rough dirt floor to her and knelt down to examine the prisoner.

Running his hands over her prone body, he tasted bile. So many bruises... cuts... all revealed by the torn fabric of her T-shirt and a brown jacket. He moved the coat's open front panels away from her torso, praying she didn't have any broken bones or major internal injuries which would make getting the fuck out of here next to impossible. Though he'd carry her out if necessary.

Blood stained her shirt just above the swell of her full breasts. Damn. He clasped the fabric at her collarbone to inspect the damage. Suddenly her shoulder muscles tensed and she kneed him in the balls.

Stars burst behind his eyes and pain shafted through his entire body. Holy mother of God. He bit back a yell and hurried to grab her, whispering in English. "Cool it. I'm here to help."

"Leave me the fuck alone," she rasped, pushing herself away from him. "You'll mess up everything if you interfere now."

What the hell? He glanced into her chocolate brown eyes—what little he could see of them given the swelling. "You should have thought of that before you let yourself get captured."

"I didn't let myself get captured, someone set me up." She lifted her chin and shot him a piercing glance. "But I didn't go to the trouble of planting you here to have you screw things up in some misguided attempt to rescue me."

JONAH ROCKED BACK on his heels and rubbed his brow. "You planted me here?"

Danielle Segal heard the shock in his low voice while he scrutinized her with those fake brown eyes —eyes she'd remembered as striking blue as he held hers during a wild night of raw, awesome sex--until slowly recognition dawned in the depths of his gaze.

"Dani?" he asked incredulously. "I—how? What

the hell are you doing here? I thought you were a secretary."

She smiled ruefully and her cracked lip burned. "Personal Assistant." They'd never exchanged last names. Just a crazy hook up, but still, he'd made her feel incredible. She'd thought maybe they could see each other again until he'd been so glad about her fake civilian career. "A cover story in between assignments. Sorry." Turned out Jonah wanted a nice, normal woman.

And Danielle was anything but normal.

"That why you never woke me up to say goodbye?"

That, and she'd already been down that road with her last serious boyfriend. She had no intention of going through another relationship of any kind with a man who didn't accept her choices.

"Didn't want to complicate your life." She'd left quietly after the top brass at her secret agency cut her week off short with urgent news about her uncle. "Looks like I've complicated it after all. I didn't know you'd be assigned to this operation."

"I volunteered because of..."

"Sandy," she said.

"How did you know?"

"Did a little research. I'm sorry," she said, meaning it. "I honestly didn't know you'd lost someone important. That you'd hated the idea of any woman you hooked up with being in a dangerous profession again. I'd never have gone to bed with you if I had." But man. Even now, here in this cell, tingles of awareness zipped through her, almost overriding the pain pulsing in every inch of her body.

The pain she welcomed. The insane reaction of her body to Jonah. Not so much.

"This operation is hosed," he said. "We'll figure out how to untangle this mess after I get you out of here."

"You mean if… maybe you shouldn't try. Let me make the sacrifice for the good of the world."

He scrubbed his face, then held her gaze. "You know what they'll do to you if I don't get you out of here."

"Yes." Unspeakable acts. Torture. Rape. A brutal death. "But important lives are at stake. Lives that are more important than mine."

"Bullshit. I won't let you die here."

"My Uncle Abarron… countless others could get killed if El Muhunnad carries out their plot to destroy my uncle's weapons' manufacturing factories." He'd literally saved her life after a suicide bomber had killed her parents. She refused to let her uncle down.

"You'll accomplish more alive than dead."

"As will you."

He took her battered hands in his strong ones, smoothed his thumbs over the scrapes. "Then I'd better be as good as my commander says and get you out, Dani," he said.

His gentle touch wove into her skin, threaded deep into her, making her nerves fire with need. The tenderness of his voice, his vow to bring her out of this nightmare, undid her in ways she'd never expected to happen again. At least not with Jonah.

She inhaled a deep breath, lassoed the need and desire into submission before she made a total idiot of herself and revealed both to him. "I don't doubt your abilities," she whispered. "Once we're out of here, I'll explain everything."

Noise echoed outside the small, dank room. "Shit. My partner's coming," Jonah said softly, but then again with greater urgency. "Lay low. I'll handle him."

Her mouth dried and every blow she'd taken on earlier pummeled her again. She obeyed immediately, rolling back into a fetal, prone position and feigning an unconscious state. Still, she kept her mind focused on the conversation ensuing between Jonah and the other guard. Heard the insults and the laughter when the other one said they wouldn't wait till the bruises faded before taking her.

And then killing her.

Fear coiled low and dread turned the blood in her veins into a slow moving sludge. Though she had always known she could end up in this position and had prepared her mind for the possibility, the reality of being compromised paled in comparison. But she had to save her uncle. He'd been her only family after they had killed her parents.

And he'd helped her become the warrior she was today. First, by teaching her everything she needed to know about her Israeli history along with all the fighting skills she needed to win a physical contest. Finally, after she'd completed her mandatory military requirement with the Israeli Defense Forces, he'd introduced her to her current commander who ran covert operations all over the world and had put Danielle in the field at the helm of the Israeli head-quarters.

When she wasn't out saving the world, she lived at the vineyard which housed the secret headquarters. Or she'd hit the clubs and bars in Jerusalem to blow off steam.

Which had put her smack into Jonah's sights while he was on leave. And his bed... She squeezed her eyes as images of being with him flashed again.

After several minutes of listening to the bantering between the men outside her holding cell, the raucous laughter dimmed and transformed to low voices. She couldn't make out what Jonah said to his partner, but several minutes later, footfalls on the hard ground followed by door hinges creaking and the echo of the bolts locking sounded. She waited several more minutes before opening her eyes to check the cell.

Alone. Finally. For now.

She rolled over and pushed her back against the wall again, listening for any sign of the other terrorists. Silence, other than the occasional murmur of movement outside the prison walls. Breathing carefully, she checked her hidden pocket in the lining of her ripped jacket.

The tension tightening her muscles eased when her fingers reached the micro communication device she'd stashed inside. It had been created specifically by her agency's technology guru and one third the size of a typical smart phone. She didn't dare retrieve it to contact headquarters. Not yet. Not when she didn't know who had betrayed her.

However, if Jonah managed to rescue her without getting them both slaughtered, it'd come in handy after they escaped. Then she'd use it to contact the few people she still trusted including the woman who'd recruited her for her covert operations' team. And she'd touch base with her commander's enigmatic, elusive counterpart known only as Dimitri.

She pushed the device deeper into her concealed pocket, then did a quick self-assessment of her injuries, running her hands over her sore, but not broken ribs. Bastards had done a number on her entire body--it'd take a while for the bruising to fade and the lacerations to heal.

But she hadn't spent hours training to let a few scrapes and raw skin stop her from attaining her end goal. And, from the determined look she'd seen earlier in Jonah's fake brown gaze, she believed he'd act on his decision to get her out of here. Once he accomplished his objective, they'd switch tactics and regroup to work together toward stopping El Muhunnad.

Jonah would be her partner. Her equal in every way. But not permanently.

Danielle retied her half-torn laces on her combat boots and tucked her shirt into her waistband, then stretched her arms over her head and flexed her fingers. Stretching her legs in front of her and twisting from left to right repetitively, she kept her eyes glued to the closed prison door.

She'd have to deal with the renewed zings zipping through her skin when she ran the mission with him. And that would be a significant amount of up close and personal time.

Moments later, her would-be rescuer and sexy weekend fling stepped into the room and hurried to her side. "We've got to move now or we'll never get out," he said, helping her stand. "I assume you know how to use this." Jonah handed her a Russian Yarygin pistol.

She tucked the sidearm in the back of her pants. "You assume correctly," she said.

"Put these on." He tossed male clothing to her and a head covering. "Follow my lead. Period. We've got one shot, then all bets are off."

"Understood." She dressed and covered her head

and face with the shemag, leaving her eyes exposed. Retrieving her gun from her waistband, she followed him toward the door. "You sure you can pull this off?" Danielle asked, cocking her weapon.

A muscle jumped in his jaw as he guided her into the corridor outside the jail cell. "Better to take the risk and die trying to escape than to have them torture you," he said under his breath. "But I won't let that happen."

"Good," Danielle said. "Then we'll get out of here as a team. That's the only way we won't blow this op." She'd focus on the mission, not the man moving ahead of her despite how he'd reignited some serious female hormone action.

CHAPTER 2

Danielle scanned the dark corridor. "Where's your partner in crime?"

"Passed out cold." Jonah nodded toward an alcove. "Slipped him a roofie. Worked instantly."

"Good thinking," she said, figuring he had access to the date rape drug via his current companions. They'd use any method at their disposal to trap someone. "What's your plan?"

"Act natural. The clothes are from my roommate —also dead to the world for the time being." Jonah indicated the passageway leading to the outside. "We're snagging the Toyota truck they brought you in and exiting the compound. If anyone stops us, I'll do the talking. As far as they know, I'm heading into the village to get supplies." He didn't waste time standing around while he talked, moving through the corridor with her keeping pace.

Every muscle screamed in agony—and pain ricocheted through her ribs. She gulped in air while
staying close to Jonah and matching his long strides.
The stench of urine she'd inhaled for hours faded as
they approached a dimly lit room located near the
main entrance.

Three men holding AK-12 Russian issue rifles
straightened when they entered the space. Danielle's
adrenaline spiked, sending pinpricks into her fingertips and crawling over her scalp with a thousand
insects.

The largest one approached them and asked in
Dari about the prisoner's status.

"She's still unconscious and won't be a problem,"
Jonah lied. "I've got new orders to go to Ak Bolmaytu
and pick up more firearms and machine guns at the
village's drop point. The key fob still in the truck?"

The insects crawling through her skull doubled.
She shot a glance at her worn combat boots, itched to
run when the frayed hem of the shelwar kameez
tunic slide over the scuffed black leather tops. If the
guards suspected anything, and the fob wasn't in the
truck, they'd get hauled back into the cells and prison
walls would be the last place she'd see before she
died.

"Why are you going with him?" the guard
asked her.

Those thousands of insects made a three-sixty
revolution, zipped down her spine to the base of her

back, lassoed around her midriff and into her gut. Fear, raw and primal, grasped her by the throat. If she said one word, they'd know right away she wasn't a man. No amount of male clothing could disguise her female voice.

"He's riding shotgun. Just in case the enemy infidels are patrolling our territory," Jonah answered without missing a beat. "Got to go before sunup or we'll lose our opportunity to smuggle the stash to the compound." He stepped around the guard and she moved right behind him.

The door was two feet away. Two feet from freedom… she hoped.

"Wait," the guard called. "I'm confirming these weapons' run with our commander."

"Go ahead, but make it fast. We haven't got all night."

Jonah stopped, and she bumped into him. "Sorry," she said on auto pilot.

The other guards pushed away from the wall as the first man made a grab for Danielle, catching her by the arm. She wrestled free, heard Jonah fire shots at the men bolting toward them. Grabbing her gun, she raced to follow him and give him top cover, shooting an oncoming terrorist between the eyes before he stopped Jonah with a bullet of his own.

Adrenaline pumped, but she kept cool, and continued shooting while making her way to the door that led to their potential freedom. "That fucking key fob better be in there," she yelled.

Another man rushed them when they got outside. A knife blade reflected the moonlight. He lunged at Jonah, who dodged the flashing steel then shot his assailant. "Hurry," he shouted, opening the truck's driver side door.

Bullets rained down from the top of the compound as she dived into the opposite side while the engine started. The truck sped up, and they careened through the gate with two other Toyotas in pursuit. The iron scent of blood filled the truck's passenger cabin. The side mirror shattered outside her window and more bullets pinged off the sideboard. She ducked, then snaked her arm out the window and fired back. "Don't stop," Danielle commanded, while firing the last of her bullets, hitting the front wheels of both vehicles.

The trucks veered off the small road, sliding off the ledge and into the ravine below.

"Good work."

She heard the respect in his voice. Warmth seeped into her weary muscles, making them go slack for a moment. "Thanks," she said. "Same to you." She needed no one's approval, but garnering it from Jonah made her like him all the more. If only…

The truck bumped over rocks and dipped into grooves, bouncing her back and forth in her seat. She clung to the worry-handle with one hand while still scanning the road behind them to search for more oncoming trucks.

"Who do you work for? Israeli Defense Force or Mossad?"

"Neither." She squeezed the worry handle a bit more tightly. "I'm an agent for C.R.U.SH."

"What's crush stand for?"

"Covert Rescuers Undercover Shield. And it's a term used when harvesting grapes for wine," she said. "We have secret headquarters housed all over the world in different wineries."

"Crazy. Never heard of them."

"Great. Then we're succeeding at keeping off the radar. A plus in my line of work."

He laughed, and the sound echoed in the truck's cab. "So you're a spy," he said. "Like James Bond?"

"I prefer to think of myself as Wonder Woman without all the superpowers," she said, still keeping her eyes on the road ahead.

"I must have missed your whip during our night together."

She grinned, grateful for the momentary reprieve and for the easy conversation. "No. But CRUSH does have a lot of fun gadgets and cool tech. We're a separate entity spread all over the world. Sometimes we join forces with the regular military. Most of the time, we run our own ops. When I approached your commander with my idea, he went for it, but I didn't know he'd plant you in the terrorist cell." Danielle took a quick look at his profile and her pulse ratcheted up a notch. Blood dripped down his cheek from a nasty gash. "You've been injured."

"Yeah, fucking guy cut me," he said. "Hurts like hell, but now my mother will be able to tell me apart from my brother Jacob."

"There's two of you?"

"Only one like me," he said with a hint of humor in his tone. "And I'm the better looking twin."

"Ha. I bet your brother uses that line too."

"Not anymore. He's in Montana. Just got hitched." He grimaced when the truck hit another groove and bounced them again. "Not sure if Jacob's going to do another tour of duty, but I'd sure as hell like another one."

"I hear you. Nothing better than getting out in the field and kicking butt."

"I can think of a few other things better than kicking bad asses to the curb."

"True." Too bad he wasn't interested in being with her that way again because of her chosen profession. Sure, she'd had her share of on-again, off-again relationships, but none had come close to attracting her so strongly. "But those things aren't on the agenda right now. We've got to contact your commander and get to CRUSH's safe house in Kabul. Plan our next move."

More blood trailed down his cheek, and he swiped it away. "Agreed."

"But first, I'll take care of that knife wound before you get gangrene from that nasty headgear," she said. "Once we're in Kabul, I'll get the agency's on-site doctor to treat it properly." Then they'd go forward with a new plan. One that didn't include acting on things far better than kicking enemy butt.

JONAH GRIPPED the steering wheel and maneuvered the truck through another hairpin curve. "We have got no first aid supplies in this truck." The road leveled out when they reached the bottom of the mountain and he continued driving through the desert. "You sure you know what you're doing?" Most likely she did considering how on point she'd been during their escape.

"I've handled worse." She ripped her tunic, then pulled three decent sized lengths of the fabric free. "Take off the shemag so I can check the damage to your face."

One handed, he complied while gripping the steering wheel with the other. "How bad is it?"

She unbuckled her seatbelt and scooted closer. "You'll want my doctor to clean the edges," she said while pressing the first round of fabric onto his face. "But don't worry. The damage won't ruin your stellar looks. Though you could use a bath." She applied more pressure, holding the fabric in place while winding another strip over his head and under his chin until she tucked the end into the side.

"You and me both," he said without thinking. Her touch, strong and careful, did more than make his face feel better. Hell, it sent a serious rush of blood race south.

Her breath hitched. "We'll squeeze a shower in after we arrive at the safe house." She retreated to her side and strapped herself in again.

He focused on the road ahead, determined to keep his mind out of the proverbial gutter. His cheek still burned, but the makeshift bandage Dani had applied to his face had stemmed the flow of blood.

"We'll want to burn these rags."

"No kidding," she said. "They reek like they've been worn by the dead."

Jonah clenched the wheel tighter while suppressing a laugh. He didn't want to admit it, but he'd liked Dani from the get-go. Since she'd vanished without bothering to say goodbye, she'd also been the star of many late night fantasies he'd indulged in. Then she'd been a sexy PA, not a spy for a covert agency. But the current addition, tough with a solid core and amazing combat skills, garnered his respect and generated some serious hard ass wishing for more hot, sweaty nights with her.

Do not go there, mentally. She's not right for you. And this gig is only temporary. Period.

Still, he couldn't deny his awareness of her... nor

could he pretend he hadn't seen her whiskey-colored eyes darken when he first locked his gaze on hers.

Starlight pin-pricked the sky in the horizon, forming constellations. Ahead he could see Kabul glowing in the distance. The river's scents of algae, mud and fish wafted into the truck's passenger cabin. They reminded him of home where he'd spent his summers hiking, swimming and riding the trails in his four wheeler with his brothers right on his tail.

"As soon as we're in satellite range, we'll contact your commander," she said after several beats of silence in the still night air.

"He might want to bring me in to debrief me," Jonah said.

"Not likely. CRUSH will handle the debrief and send the intel to him through secure networks."

"But he's still my commander? Why not?"

"We made all the arrangements through our central command in Virginia. He's known our leader since she was a teenager and worked with her mother when she led CRUSH. We'll send him the details of this op and let him interface with the Pentagon as necessary." She motioned to the dark desert sands on either side of the truck. "Serene out here for now. Reminds me of the road trips my folks used to take me on."

He heard the wistfulness in her voice and caught the slight sheen glimmering in her profile's swollen eye when he slanted a glance her way. "You're close to them."

"I was close to them until a suicide bomber blew up the coffee shop they frequented," she said. Her voice was sharp as a knife's edge.

"Damn, Dani," Jonah said gently after a second of silence. "I'm sorry. I can't imagine losing my folks. I guess I'd be all over fighting the bad guys if that had happened to me."

"You're fighting the bad guys," she said matter-of-factly. "And thanks for keeping it real. Too many people think they can sugarcoat loss with platitudes. Nothing can bring them back."

"I know. But they must have been great parents," he said. "After all, you're pretty damn great."

"They were amazing. Not that we didn't fight," she said. "But I never doubted their love for me. They made me believe I could be anything, do anything I wanted in life. And they supported me 100 percent no matter what I wanted to try."

His heart squeezed and pain lanced behind his breastbone. How had she'd survived losing them? "I expect they'd be very proud of everything you're doing now," he said, catching the first glimmers of city life in the distance.

"Most likely I'd have done something different if they hadn't been killed when I was fifteen, but yes. I like to think so."

"What would you have done instead?"

"I loved traveling. Discovering new things. Maybe I'd have become a tour guide or run my own travel service. But...," her voice trailed off.

"Life threw you a curve ball," he said, not wanting to dredge up more sad memories. Better to focus on the tasks they faced now. "Now you're a world traveling kick butt spy."

"Exactly."

Kabul's city glow grew brighter. "We should be in range now," he said, slowing down a notch.

"Hold on." Beside him, she slipped her arm into the tunic's sleeve, then pulled what looked like a miniature version of his iPhone from within the folds.

"Cool gadget. You had that all along?"

"Yes. But I didn't dare risk using it before now." She extracted a small headphone piece and inserted it into her ear, then squeezed a button on the side. After a few seconds, she spoke. "Someone compromised us. Operation protocol to keep our mission in action."

Minutes later, after relaying her capture and subsequent rescue, she popped out the headset piece and gave it to Jonah. "He wants to talk to you."

"I see you've met our contact," Jonah's commanding officer said without preamble. "Excellent job getting her out of the compound."

Man. He couldn't be more all out of fucks than

right now. "Code word." Jonah asked per their arranged communication protocol.

"Saber Stop."

"Affirmed," Jonah said. "What are my orders?"

"Continue the covert op with CRUSH's agency. Danielle's the lead on this," his commander said. "You realize if you're taken, we can't admit you're one of ours."

"Affirmative."

"Excellent. Report back to me for a full debriefing after you've stopped El Muhunnad."

"Yes, sir." He gave the device back to Dani. "Looks like we're a team until we complete the op."

"Good. I can't think of anyone I'd rather work with right now."

Kabul's skyscrapers drew closer, and the road became more passable with each passing mile. "We're almost at the city limits," he said. "My commander's green light means using CRUSH's resources, not mine. So guide me in."

"Merge onto the Kabul-Kandahar highway in ten kilometers, then we'll head into the city via Qargha," she said. "That'll get us to the right area."

Jonah kept his gaze on the road, scanning for Taliban and other potential threats. "Got it," he said, then eased onto the highway connecting Kabul to Kandahar where the traffic picked up.

The highway needed a ton of repairs, but he'd driven over the potholes and cracked pavement so many times he practically had all the pitfalls memorized. A convoy of canvas-covered trucks ahead slowed his progress to a crawl. Damn traffic could screw up their escape, but he spotted the exit sign a hundred yards ahead, took it, finally free of the logjam.

After avoiding another jagged pothole, he glanced her way and caught her wetting her lips. Though they'd been split by a fist, the damage didn't detract from the perfection of her mouth. A mouth he'd had on him in all the right places. A mouth he'd love to kiss... and once more experience the sensation of her licking her way down his torso... He shook his head. He might want her again, but the complications of acting on the desire outweighed the benefits of acting on his attraction.

CHAPTER 3

"Air strike must have happened today," Jonah said as they drove through streets filled with rubble and concrete piles of debris. "What if your safe house is part of the damage?"

Danielle glanced at Jonah's profile, read concern in his set jaw as he gripped the steering wheel. "Not a possibility. We're not above ground and we reinforce our walls with titanium steel. It'd take a monster strike to bring it down," she said. "My uncle conferred with CRUSH's central command for years to make this place accessible for our agency."

"He's with CRUSH?"

"Only in an advisory capacity." She looked away from Jonah, leaned her head against the passenger side's window to stare into the city's wasted depths. "He's the one who recommended I talk to the agency's top leader after I finished my mandatory military tour."

"And you never once thought about trying a different career option."

"Never." She licked her lips, then pressed her fingers to her throat and rubbed the vulnerable hollow. "I've spent the better part of the last thirteen years trying to make something, anything, good come out of the most horrible day of my life." Yet, the tragedy continued to haunt her.

"You're a fighter through and through," he said. "Can't blame you for wanting to make a wrong a right."

"I'll never stop fighting, Jonah." Which made her the wrong woman for him based on his assertions.

"Trust me," he said. "I understand."

"I know."

Suddenly, memories crowded her mind with the specters of her past. Her uncle's rage and her own regret... all the anguish squeezed her heart with phantom fingers.

"Uncle Abarron is the only family I've got," Danielle said, still rubbing her throat, comforting and encouraging herself to go on despite the despair echoing in her brain. "I won't lose him too."

"I won't let you."

"Glad I've got you in my corner," she said, then pointed to a side street. "Take a left here."

Jonah complied and maneuvered the truck

through the narrow passage, bouncing over bump and grooves while avoiding rusty cars with cracked windshields, some of them missing tires and bumpers.

Seeing the destruction brought more memories. Memories that shamed her… fed the guilt underpinning every action she'd taken since then.

She'd been a total brat the day they had killed her parents, not wanting to go with them for breakfast at their favorite coffee shop. Still smarting from a bad ending to her date the night before… still angry at her father interrupting her first real kiss. Even now, she remembered the horrible things she'd said to her parents before she'd stomped into her room and slammed her door.

Teenage drama. Nothing unusual there. But then she'd lost them in an instant. A lump lodged in her throat and pain stabbed behind her ribcage. She'd never be able to apologize or tell her mom and dad she loved them.

She straightened in her seat, took in the men carrying rifles while traversing the rooftops ahead. A mangy dog with matted fur darted in front of the truck and Jonah braked to avoid hitting the poor, starving mutt. "I'm not digging this sector of Kabul," he said when they reached a crossroad. "Too many potential threats."

"We're safer here than downtown. Trust me," she said. "Take a left here."

He peered down the dark corridor. "You're sure you know where you're going?"

She stifled the urge to roll her eyes. Oh, just wait until he saw what her agency had hidden in plain sight. "Trust me," she said again. "Turn here. We're almost at the safe house."

"Sure thing," he said, then turned onto the street lined with two and three-story stone buildings. He continued driving as the road grew even more narrow and rows of clothes hung between the buildings, flags of normalcy when nothing could be further from the truth. Here and there the ravages of bombs and missile strikes punctuated the serene night views.

"Will this insanity ever end?" he asked. "I guess that's why I keep signing up for new tours of duty. Hoping one day we'll stop the bloodshed for good."

"Same here." Too bad her commitment to CRUSH wasn't a factor he considered optimum when dating. Didn't matter. She couldn't let her wishes screw with her mindset. "I'm contacting my second in command, Esther. Telling her we're coming in." She retrieved her micro smart phone while talking to him.

"Danielle, where are you?" Esther asked immediately. "We've been frantic to find you."

"Operation Eagle Blade is compromised," she said without missing a beat. "We're coming in."

"We?"

"The SEAL the military planted rescued me from

El Muhunnad's compound after the terrorists discovered my identity," Danielle said without elaborating. No one was above suspicion, not even her second-in-command. "ETA is ten minutes."

"You've got it. But what about your uncle?"

"He's in Frankfurt preparing his speech for the World Philanthropy Awards Ceremony." He'd flown there against Danielle's wishes, but her uncle bowed to no one and refused to let terrorist threats guide his actions.

"Our Russian contact, Dimitri, is there. We'll use him and his people to make sure no one gets to Abarron."

"The Russian is not me." No way would she let a stranger try to convince her obstinate uncle to lie low until CRUSH neutralized the threat. Plus, other than Jonah, she trusted no one anymore. Not after an insider betrayed her identity to her captors. "We'll need passports, western clothing, the works."

"Danielle."

Oh, she recognized the tone so well. Chastisement and worry rolled into the older woman's voice. But Esther didn't have a debt to pay that had started the day Danielle's parents died. "You know I'm right," she said with extra determination in her voice. "Focus on rooting out the mole. We can't afford more security breaches."

She gave additional instructions in Hebrew before hanging up.

"You're in charge of this unit. Impressive."

And another reason she was forbidden fruit where he was concerned. "A lot of our branches have female commanders." She tucked her device back in her jacket and repositioned her tunic to cover her body again. "That a problem for you?" She'd like to think not given everything that had happened since they'd captured her.

"Hell no. My mom and sister would have my hide if I didn't respect a woman's authority."

"Good to know." The safe house came into view. Looking at the building from the outside, people would assume five homes existed in the three story row which took up an entire block. They had zero inkling about the vast complex hidden in the ground below. "Park behind the blue Toyota Corolla when we get to the next block. We'll go on foot from there."

"Works for me." He pulled into the spot, then turned off the engine. "We've got to scuttle this truck."

"My team will take care of it." She unbuckled her seatbelt, then opened her door, stepped outside into the crisp night air, then rounded the vehicle to the sidewalk where Jonah stood.

He gave her another gun and the extra clip of bullets. "Here."

Danielle snapped the clip in place. "Let's go. We're safe here, but only until the mole leaks this intel too."

Wind whipped the headgear from her hair and

she clutched it to her throat as she moved beside Jonah toward stairs that led to the second door in the safe-house. Climbing the stairs, she wracked her brain for any clue about who might have blown out her cover. Just one problem: she'd recruited everyone in her branch which meant someone she'd trusted had betrayed her.

JONAH CHECKED the vicinity for any unusual activity. Other than another mangy mutt yipping in the distance, nothing. When they arrived at the door, Dani pressed the intercom. "Private Label Misty Mountain Blanc," she said after the night guard answered.

What the fuck? "You're ordering wine?"

"Just getting us where we need to be," she said as the door opened. "Come on."

They stepped inside the small foyer with a modern metal door at the opposite side. Dani stepped in front of a facial recognition machine built into the panel. "Got to scan my retinas before they let us in."

Curious, he leaned in to check out the system. The state-of-the-art computer technology rivaled his government's identification programs. Sure, he'd seen top-secret shit as a SEAL in the field, but this was beyond anything he had experienced. "Some high-tech equipment," he said while waiting for Dani's retinas to get cleared for entry.

"You haven't seen anything yet."

Another click and the entry's floor descended, then a door swung open to let them into a cavernous room filled with desks, people monitoring a bank of large screens on the opposite wall. He rocked back on his heels. "This is quite the setup."

"This is one of many headquarters around the world, though I prefer running things from the winery in Israel." She removed the head covering while they walked across the concrete floor to an office. "Follow me."

Walking with her, he checked out CRUSH's unique Coat of Arms. It'd been etched on all the office doors which lined the main room's perimeter and painted black on a purple placard above the satellite screens.

She pushed open a door. "Come in. We haven't got time to spare."

Jonah removed the cloth covering his head. His cheek still burned beneath the makeshift bandage Dani had applied to the knife wound. "Shit," he hissed.

She moved to stand in front of him, then frowned as she examined his face. "You've bled through the bandage. Let's get the worst of the dirt off you before you get an infection." Dani tilted her head toward another door. "Go on. Bedroom and en suite bath is through there. I've got supplies to patch you up. We'll have medical check you out in the morning."

"Sounds good."

He went into the bedroom where he found neatly folded clean clothes for him and Dani on the full size bed. Swiftly, he headed into the bathroom where he stripped off his desert crap and, after glancing around, deposited them into a hamper located inside a utilitarian closet.

Austere yes. But he inhaled Dani's aroma... a light, crisp scent he'd gotten a full dose of months earlier. Damn. She'd been fun, flirtatious...

He turned around to grab his check his face out when the bathroom door opened again and Dani stepped in with first aid bag. "Sit down now. I want to disinfect your wound."

The woman he'd rescued from the compound didn't come close to the one he'd met months ago. Nor did she act like the one he'd gotten to know during their escape from El Muhunnad.

This new version—all hard edges, focused on the tasks they'd face— take-charge and battle ready— intrigued him in different ways.

"Sure, but please... be gentle." He raised an eyebrow and winced as pain shot through his nerves.

She lifted the first aid kit. "Bathroom. Now."

He complied, and she followed him in. Within minutes, she had removed the makeshift bandage with medical tweezers and thrown it away. He shifted on the toilet seat while she pressed a sterile gauze against the wound. She was close. So close, he could see gold striations in her dark brown eyes. And every time she moved to do something her legs brushed against his torso.

"You're lucky. The blade didn't go as deep as I thought." She pressed a sterile gauze against the wound. "Doesn't look like you'll need stitches, but we'll have the doctor look at it tomorrow morning before we take off for Frankfurt. Here. Hold this while I get the antiseptic." She took his hand and pressed it on the gauze.

Lust whirled through his body, hot and laced with raw desire. One touch. A simple connection. Skin-to-skin. And bam. Instant craving. And his reaction now had been the same the first time he laid eyes on her in the sports bar. But Jonah liked his women to stick and not dash at the first opportunity to deep dive into a dangerous situation. Not after what happened to Sandy.

At least he did before this crazy reunion. Now confusion rolled through him, eroding his resolve one wave at a time.

"I got this," he said.

Her fingers trembled against his, and then she blinked. "O… Of course," she said, pulling her hand away as fast as if a bee had stung her.

Until that second, she'd been cool as the winter

wind blowing through the mountains surrounding his hometown in Montana. Now he knew better.

"So Dani," he said as she withdrew the antiseptic from the first aid bag, "am I bunking here with you?"

The antiseptic dropped to the floor and brown liquid splashed on his shoes. "Shit," she said, kneeling to pick the bottle up. "No. We're just figuring out where to put you. Every available room is taken other than mine."

"Just give me a pallet and I'll sleep on the floor." Jonah hissed as she dabbed the antiseptic onto his cut. "Damn. Could you go a little easy on the Betadine?"

"Sorry."

"You could blow on it… make me feel better," he couldn't resist teasing to see if he could coax out her lighter side.

Her breath hitched and her nostrils flared. "I'll tell someone to make you a bed on the floor." She withdrew a few butterfly bandages from the kit and applied them to his cheek. "These'll hold you together until tomorrow."

"Thanks. You want to take the first shower, or should I?" he asked though he would prefer to shower together. And, from the look gleaming in her eyes, she remembered all too well their last shower.

Up close and personal and hotter than the water cascading over their bodies.

His cock hardened, desired one thing… to be

buried deep inside her. The heat that had flared between them months ago, had never fully evaporated, rushed back with extra fire. Looked like Dani's had too. Though she attempted to resume a just-business demeanor with her matter-of-fact tone of voice, she failed to fool him. Not when her nipples strained against the fabric of her torn shirt.

Dani cleared her throat, then replaced all the items in the first aid kit. "Go ahead," she said. "I've got to debrief with the team first." Then she pushed away from the counter and exited the room, closing the door with a sharp bang on her way out.

"PASSPORTS ARE HERE," Esther said when Danielle reached the command center the following morning. "The jet's fueled and ready to go." She tucked a curling gray strand of hair behind her ear.

"Wardrobe? Hotel reservations?" Danielle asked.

"Packed and done," Esther said, sliding the passports across her desk, then looked at Jonah who stood beside Danielle "Jack and Diane Martin. Dossiers are in the briefcase. You can study them on your way to Germany."

"God knows we'll have plenty of time to memorize the details." The flight would take well over ten hours. Fortunately, the jet had a bedroom. And chairs capable of stretching into a sleeping cocoon.

Which, after the restless night she'd had tossing and turning in her bed while she tried to block the delicious scent of the man sleeping on the floor next to her, was highly necessary. She needed her wits operating at 100 percent throughout the rest of the mission.

Indulging in fantasies that featured the gorgeous SEAL working with her? Off-limits.

Jonah picked his passport up and flipped it open. "Looks good," he said, then rubbed his right cheek where the in-house doctor had cleaned up the jagged edges of his knife wound, then used precise, deep dissolvable stitching and joined the skin together with more butterfly pieces of adhesive tape. Just a thin scar would remain after the wound healed.

"If anyone asks about your face, you got that nasty cut after slipping on a wet rock during a hike in the Sierra Nevada's," Esther said, then stood and pointed to the main com area. "Check out the recent satellite feeds. Things are getting interesting."

"Any clue about the assassin or his whereabouts?"

"Not yet, but one of our operatives followed three members of El Muhunnad to Kabul. They stocked up on weapons, but they didn't return to the compound. They're still holed up in a house."

"Train a satellite on them. I want to know where they are every second of the day until we neutralize this threat." She pocketed her passport. "Jonah, contact your commander and tell him we leave at

1800 hours. Let's go." She grabbed the briefcase and made her way to the satellite screens.

"You've got your satellites trained on multiple locations," he said as they entered the common area. "Almost have El Muhunnad's compound in your sights."

"The only one I care about is the Frankfurt feed."

He nodded. "I understand."

Still moving toward the banks of desks, she scoped the downtown hotel the satellites had zoomed in on. Five black Mercedes Benz's pulled into the valet lane in front of the opulent lobby's doors. Beside her, Jonah withdrew the communicator he'd gotten from requisitions and contacted his commanding officer.

"Your uncle staying there?" he asked when he finished giving his intel.

He'd debriefed with her team and the information proved useful. Now they had the names of several weapons' suppliers and their meet sites.

"Yes. He's giving a speech at the Grandhotel Rüdesheim and brokering a weapons deal with the European Union." She stopped walking when they reached the first row of desks where a slender thirtyish woman with a white-blonde pixie cut entered data into a high-tech computer.

"This is one of the best tech geniuses' in the world, Marily Kohn. She's responsible for hooking me up with this." She withdrew the gadget she'd used to communicate with the safe house.

"Remember to take it easy with the hardware," Marily said. "That's the third one you've gotten since we rolled them out."

"Hey, how am I supposed to stop a tank from smashing these things?" she asked before slipping the device back in her pocket. "You got any other cool toys for us to bring along on this mission?"

"A few things," Marily said, shooting Jonah a quick glance. "Does he have clearance to use them?"

"He's part of our team." Temporarily until he rejoined his SEAL team. But for now, he was hers. "So yes."

"A team of two," Jonah said.

A fake married team. Something she'd have to deal with every night from now until they stopped the assassin. Up close and personal. Alone. Her nipples tightened into buds just thinking about everything he'd done the last time they'd been alone, up close and personal.

She inhaled a deep breath to control her reaction, willing her rebellious hormones to stand down. Bad move. He smelled so good, clean and masculine and uniquely him. More desire unfurled low, heating her face, blazing a path through her veins into her breasts and between her thighs.

He lowered his gaze, centering on her chest, then

drifting back to meet her eyes with his smoldering as if the fire burning inside her had arced over to him.

She didn't break the connection. She Stood there like a sex-starved idiot, unable to tear her glance away from his drop-dead gorgeous face with those luscious, bronze freckles. Freckles she'd licked all the way down to... oh yeah. His masculine appeal had ratcheted up several thousand notches since he'd ditched his disguise and scrubbed the desert off his body.

Focus on the mission. Nothing else matters. Once this is over, he'll return to the SEALs and I'll move on. I've done it before and I can do it again.

With an iron will, she finally broke their gaze. "Yes. A trial. Period," she said, then stepped closer to the screens. "Marily, close in on the license plates."

"On it."

"No identification," Jonah said from behind her. "Can you get a better shot? I think I see something on the first Mercedes."

"Sure thing."

Moments later, a black mass of disgust and grief fused behind her breastbone, making her heartbeat pound. "Russians. Their favorite cars and the diplomatic tags scream their identities." Not the good kind like Dimitri and his agents. No. These people used every method at their disposal to create worldwide chaos. Arming terrorists. Maybe even arming her parents' killer.

"Not surprised," Jonah said. "They're everywhere."

She watched the screen and heaved a sigh when her uncle, flanked by his bodyguards, exited the hotel and entered his limo. "Uncle Abarron is too stubborn for his own good," she said. "If the Russians are involved, then we've got a bigger problem to fix." But she'd leave the bulk of those missions to the woman who'd brought her into this undercover agency.

She glanced at the Coat of Arms hanging above the screens. Read their motto. *Courage Defies Danger.* Now more than ever she had to believe they'd beat the odds in Frankfurt and then they'd annihilate the terrorists one cell at a time. Evil existed. And always would exist given the history of the world. Still, as long as good persisted... as long as people fought corruption she had hope. And the hope, the ongoing fight for justice, had been why she'd become a CRUSH operative.

"We won't let anything happen to your uncle," Jonah said, moving to stand beside her. "And we'll stop El Muhunnad's leader."

Pressure landed on her shoulders and back, weighing heavy. She'd had other partners while out in the field, but Jonah's soft, compassionate assurance... the confidence in his voice made her think of him as more than an undercover operative. She'd known no one like him and until she'd acted on her attraction to him, she'd never been with a man who saw her truly as an equal in every way. On the battle-field. As fighters. Not lovers.

She turned to face him once more. "Yes," she said. "We will."

Electricity bounced between them and the air grew heavy, pulsing like a living entity. Around her the humming of the computers and buzzing over-head lights evaporated. And for a moment there was only him… only her… only the possibility for more.

"Danielle, the terrorists are on the move."

Marily's sharp voice sliced the attraction simmering between them. And Danielle refocused her attention on the tasks ahead, knowing neither she nor Jonah should act on their mutual craving. Their differences outweighed their similarities.

His blue eyes still glinted with awareness, dark and gleaming and all-too decadent. She turned from his piercing gaze to scan the screen in front of her to keep on top of the terrorists' intentions. "Track them." Danielle returned to the desk with Jonah close behind. Way too close. She could feel his body heat emanating from him. Her knees buckled ever so slightly, forcing her grip the back of a chair until she jettisoned her reaction. "Report every step they take. Jonah, let's gear up, then go over our tactical plan in my office."

He grabbed the attaché case she'd placed on the desk at the same time she went for it and their fingers touched, sparking another round of electricity. She snatched her hand back and tucked it into her pant pocket.

"I've got this," he said.

"Great. We'll review the contents here and during the flight," she said with feigned nonchalance, wondering if he could hear her heart drumming inside her chest.

No. She shouldn't do anything with Jonah Lawson. But she couldn't deny the truth thrumming through her veins. And despite knowing she'd risk repeating the same mistake by acting on her attraction, she wanted to in a bad way.

CHAPTER 4

CRUSH DIDN'T SKIMP on the extras. The private jet Jonah had boarded three hours earlier at 11 pm was a stellar example. A first. He'd never traveled in high style—every flight had been coach class or he'd hitched a ride on a Blackhawk helicopter and hop to an airport to catch a military plane to reach his destination. Now he reclined in a wide passenger seat, the buttery leather cushioning him while he stretched his legs in front of him.

"A guy could get used to these kinds of upscale benefits," he said. "But I think I'll stick with the SEALs. Don't want to get soft." Though he was anything but soft whenever he got within a foot of Dani.

Across from him, her breath hitched.

"CRUSH doesn't take these luxuries for granted," she said, then continued reading the schematics of the conference center where her uncle would give his speech in less than a week. "They're a necessary and efficient means to get where we're needed."

"An operation this big has got to cost tons of money to run." He glanced around the passenger cabin, took in all the extra amenities. "How do you pay for all this stuff? The safe house couldn't have been cheap to set up either?"

"Old money established the agency. Now we're hired by private entities with deep pockets and the government hires us for off-the-grid missions whenever red tape ties their hands," she said. "We've also got a major financial genius managing CRUSH's portfolio. Our headquarters are well in the black."

"How many do you have?"

"Four. A fifth is under construction in Italy," Dani said. "Most of our agents live regular lives until we assign them to a new mission. We go in. We fix the impossible. We get out. Consider joining our agency after we complete this mission. You'd be a valuable asset."

His gut tightened. Joining CRUSH would put him back in play with a woman he couldn't protect. A woman dedicated—rightfully so—to putting herself in danger. Not an option. Not after what had happened to Sandy. "Since you're so successful, I'll stick with the SEALs. They need me more than CRUSH," he said, leaning forward. Her unique aroma, tart and sweet like lemonade on a hot summer day, wafted into his senses. More than his gut reacted, making him want to dropkick his decision to avoid acting on the chemistry simmering between them.

"Certainly," she said, holding his gaze with darkening eyes. "That's your prerogative. Still glad to have you on my team for this op, particularly since I have a mole in my sector who is undermining my objectives."

Her capture, the subsequent and real possibility she could have been killed, slapped him back to reality. If he hadn't been planted in the compound, Dani would have died a horrible death. "We'll stop the terrorists," he said. "And we'll stop the mole." Leaving her without ferreting out the person who'd betrayed her didn't sit well with him. But he could only stay with her for the duration of the mission.

Somehow that rattled him more than he wanted to admit to himself. But even if he accepted her offer to jump over to CRUSH, he'd have to live with the constant fear or possibility of another tragedy occurring… especially when Dani had no desire to stop putting herself in the line of fire.

"Let's go over the schematics one more time," he said. Better to focus on the task before them and not his concern for her. That'd only lead him down a slippery slope and confuse the shit out of him even more.

"Security is tripled here and here," she said,

pointing to the main entrances and exits on the blueprints she'd spread on the console table between them.

He followed her hand movements. His groin tightened, lust arrowing hot and wild. She'd done amazing things to his dick with her hands... her mouth... *Shut it down, Lawson. Get a God damn grip on yourself.* Dousing himself with a serious dose of mental salt Peter, he pushed down the desire.

"Nothing will stop El Muhunnad from breaching the extra guards. They're stealth. And always have someone on the inside," he said. "Whoever their leader is, he's got the financial backup to bribe and recruit people."

"We've gone over this multiple times. Nothing more to do other than..." Dani paused, rubbed her neck, glancing away, then cleared her throat.

"Catch some shuteye." Man, his voice sounded like a kid going through puberty.

The jet rode over some light turbulence, pitching her forward over the console and giving him an awesome view of her cleavage. He tugged his designer shirt's collar which suddenly squeezed his throat with a vise-like grip.

She righted herself, then folded the blueprints without looking at him. But no way could she conceal the rosy blush on her chest and cheeks. "There's only one bedroom onboard," she said, tucking the paperwork into the attaché case. "But the chairs fold out into sleeping bunks."

"Sounds good." Jonah then pressed a button on his seat's side panel. The footrest rose, and the back reclined. "Definitely the best flight I've ever been on." Except he'd much rather share that bedroom with Dani than hunker down in the single bed cocoon.

"You've never flown with your famous sister?"

"No time," he said. "Too busy saving the world."

"Same here," she said, then stood. "I guess I'll turn in. We won't have much time to..."

The jet pitched left violently and threw her into his lap. He wrapped his arms around her, heard the seatbelt warning ting. "Time to what?" he asked as the captain's voice came over the intercom telling them they'd hit rough air.

She pushed up, still straddling him, and held his eyes with her chocolate brown gaze. "Sleep," she said after inhaling a breath which didn't hide her breathless voice or the rosy blush on her cheeks.

The jet hit another bad pocket, bouncing her pelvis against his groin and pressing her breasts onto his chest. Her pebbled nipples poked him through the fabric and her sexy scent filled his nostrils with every breath he inhaled. All his blood zoomed low, filling his dick until he thought he'd lose the ability to breathe at all.

Another rolling pitch moved her up and down his torso. When she didn't push away, he gripped her hips, cupped her ass to hold her steady. Damn. She had the best ass, full and curvaceous with tight muscles from her years of military training.

The captain came back on the intercom. "Sorry. That's the worst of it. You can move about the cabin freely now."

She stayed in his arms. "I'm glad that's over."

Jonah swallowed hard. "Guess we can try to get some sleep before we land," he said, though he'd rather continue holding her and then doing a lot more. His rock hard cock agreed.

She didn't break her gaze from his. "From what I can tell, sleeping is the last thing you want to do," Dani said, then licked her lips.

"How about you?" he asked, loosening his hold to give her the option of getting off him. Yeah. He wanted her. And he was damn sure she wanted him too.

Every internal objection he had to being with her jettisoned out of his brain. He respected her and the dedication she'd given to CRUSH. It mirrored his to the SEALs. And knowing she cared about the world enough to save it sure as hell made the idea of acting on all this fucking heat burning between them a stellar one even if the end result would be the same... they'd go their separate ways to fight their separate battles.

But he'd leave the choice in her court.

LONGING. An intense desire to fill the emptiness she'd called her constant companion for years ached behind her breastbone. Danielle loved being in Jonah's arms and the second he let them go slack, she missed the warmth of his embrace. But, reading the honor shining in his clear blue eyes, she realized he'd given her an out. If she wanted to take one.

She didn't.

Not when her entire body hummed to life whenever she encountered the man. Why not act on this insane attraction and get it out of her, and his, system once and for all?

"The bed's big enough for two," she said, then brushed her mouth against the vulnerable center pulsing in his throat and tasted his skin.

He groaned and hitched his hips. "Or we could stay here." He cruised his hands over her bottom, bringing her closer. "Save steps."

His hard on rubbed her core. Lust caressed the underside of her skin, beading her nipples into tight, sensitive points. Delicious sensations of heat and need pooled between her legs and spiraled into her sex, making her wet. She wanted him, craved him.

He'd had a starring role in all her fantasies for months. Now she'd put him in the lead, up close and personal.

Her clit pulsed and tingles traveled through her

body. Yes. She could do him here. Now. But she wanted more than hurried sex.

"I like your idea," she said, trailing kisses down his neck and to the other side, then moved higher to hover her lips scant millimeters from his. "But the bedroom's private. And we'll have more room to," she took his lower lip into her mouth and then released it with a pop, "screw around," she said, pushing off him to stand. Sex with Jonah had to be just that—sex, nothing more. She'd get this out of her system and after they landed in Frankfurt, everything would return to business as usual.

Jonah's lips curved into a half-smile. "You don't have to tell me twice." He exited his seat to stand in front of her. "I've wanted to be with you since the day I rescued you."

"I don't know what it is about you, Jonah." She stared into those gorgeous blue eyes, loving the desire darkening the irises. "But I haven't gotten enough of you." Yet. How could she when he ignited all her hormones into serious overdrive, giving her cravings only he'd satisfy?

"Good. You still on the pill?" he asked, holding her gaze.

"Yes," she said. "Just passed my last physical too. How about you?"

"Same status quo as last time." He closed the scant distance between them and took her hands in his. "Haven't been with anyone else either."

Knowing he hadn't been with another woman since their crazy weekend together gave her a possessive thrill. Her entire body craved his touch, his mouth. Everything he offered. Everything she wanted to claim again. "I've been too busy to fool around," she said. He'd basically ruined her for other men, but she didn't articulate the thought.

He raised his brows slightly, then he tugged her closer. "Good to know." Jonah released her hands and caressed her face, sliding his thumb pad over her mouth. "Because I can't wait to hear you cry my name again when I drive my cock into your pussy."

Arousal streaked through her veins like a savage beast, making her nipples pebble and her pussy hot, wet, aching. "I wasn't that loud."

"Oh, yeah?" Jonah moved her with him, walking backwards to the door which led to the jet's sleeping quarters. "How about we test that theory?" He stroked her lips again and then brought his hand lower to caress one of her breasts.

"Yes." She reached around him, the movement giving him easier access to her breasts, thrusting the peaks into his hands. "Let's... test... ooohhhh...," she moaned as they tumbled into the dimly lit room.

He tweaked her tender, sensitized points through her shirt's fabric, teasing them. "You were saying?"

Pleasure. Ecstasy. Wild need charged from her nipples straight to her clit. Her craving intensified, spiraled through her, blotting out all reasonable thought. Obliterated her ability to speak coherently.

She kicked the door closed while coiling her hands around his neck to anchor herself. He lowered his mouth to hers and kissed her. She expected urgency, one that matched her own... but his kiss was tender, soft and silky slow.

Too tender.

But oh how she loved the sweet glide of his tongue tangling with hers as if he was kissing her for the first time. He tasted like sin, sexy and decadent. Addictive. She opened up for him, tangling her tongue with his, hungry for more than she'd ever fully admitted to herself.

She wanted him. Body, mind, soul. She wanted all of him. Not just the wild insanity of their first time in bed, but everything else he had to offer. Even as her practical brain rebelled against her unspoken wishes, her body trembled and ached with rebellion. He was hers.

Somehow, they removed their clothing in the midst of touching each other, their heightened desire releasing in gasps and pants.

Then they fell into the king-sized bed and Jonah moved over her, his incredible, muscular body rubbing every sensitive inch of her naked skin. She clasped his broad shoulders, and he brought his hand to her core, played with her throbbing clit.

She moaned even louder. And he inhaled the

sound with his mouth, still kissing her with a sweetness she'd never expected... had never realized how much she needed until now.

He broke their kiss, stroked the damp hair from her brow and lowered his to touch it. "What's going on in that big brain of yours?"

Everything. "Nothing...," she said, seeing her reflection in his dark pupils and wondering if she could simply be the passionate woman she barely recognized in them instead of a hardened warrior she'd honed for years. "Could we just get a move on? You're taking too long." She wanted to be both, but she didn't know how to surrender total control. Maybe she could learn one day. Not tonight.

"Nope," he said, sliding his finger into her folds, then sweeping the moisture over her clit slowly. "I've waited too long to have you to do a rush job. I will make this last all night long."

Need spiraled through her, the empty, throbbing wet sex clenched, restless, aching for more. "Jonah," she moaned.

He fused his mouth to hers again, pushed a finger into her, pumping while she rode his hand. Pressure, heat, coiled. Her resistance to the promise in his words dissolved. Because she wanted to be adored, cherished by this man even if only during this flight.

CHAPTER 5

DANI HELD ONTO HIM, the scent of her shampoo and her distinct feminine musk filling his nostrils, shooting hot blood into his cock. Jonah grew harder, continuing to penetrate her mouth with his tongue, and the slick folds of her sex with his finger. Intensifying his assault on her mouth, he wanted to taste more of her... her arousal filling him with a hunger, a ravenous craving after months of self-inflicted sexual starvation.

Her liquid heat flowed onto his hand as she bucked into it, riding his caress. He plunged another finger into her hot, wet pussy, giving her what her body demanded. She clenched around them, drawing him deeper, moaning into his mouth.

Fuck. He couldn't get enough. Over and over, he drove his fingers into her while roaming his other hand to her belly. Then higher still to one luscious breast to pinch and tweak her elongated nipple between his fingers and thumb. He wanted to fuck her senseless, drive his cock into her all the way to the hilt, hear her scream his name.

But he'd meant everything he'd said to her. He hadn't known she'd disappear on him after their weekend together. Believed they'd hook up again... for more than sex... more than hot, dirty sex in every possible way.

He swallowed her moans, her breathless gasps, then broke away from her succulent, kiss-swollen lips to trail his lips down her neck... lower... and lower still until he reached her cherry red nipple. Still flicking the other bud, he licked around the aureole, smiled when her breath hitched a decibel higher, then sucked the sweet tip in.

She jerked against him, crying out. Her fingers tangled in his hair, clutched him to her breast. Her nails raked his skin, the scrape hurtling to his dick.

Man, she was fucking perfect. A lust driven haze muddled his thoughts, invading his mind with another craving he'd denied himself.

He didn't know if he'd ever find another woman like Dani. He wouldn't, shouldn't hold on to her permanently. But right now, he didn't have to worry about the future. Not when he had her beneath him, moving in tandem with him.

Jonah licked his way across her heaving chest to the twin peak to suck it into his mouth. God. She tasted sweet and tart like ripe peaches and cinnamon. He already knew the rest of her, the very essence of her, had the same flavor. Then he traced his tongue lower until he reached the apex of her thighs.

"Yes. Oh, yes." She held him between her legs, widening them to give him greater access. "I want to feel your mouth on me again," she said, raising her hips and twining her fingers through his hair.

Her arousal invaded his senses, making his mouth water. He inhaled the tangy, spicy aroma and looked at her. "I haven't forgotten how excellent you taste," he said, fucking her with his fingers and running his thumb over her twitching clit.

She parted her rosy lips and raised her hips higher. "As I recall, you're quite skilled in using your tongue to do more than talk," she said between gasps.

"You're close," he said, pushing his fingers deeper and moving them faster. "So fucking close."

Her pussy's walls clenched around him and he licked the creamy cum, loving the salty, sweet combination. He licked her clit, then sucked it into his mouth while driving his fingers into her.

She bucked her hips. "Don't stop. Oh, my… damn you're good."

His ears thundered and everything grew misty. He withdrew his fingers from her pulsating pussy and replaced them with his tongue, fucking her and drinking her juice.

She was so close he could feel her clench around him, drawing him deeper into her. Fucking fantastic. He added his fingers, flicking her clit and plunging into her wet depths over and over.

"Jonah," she screamed. "Yes. I'm..."

Her orgasm came in a rush of fluid, hot honey he sucked in until her movements slowed. Then he licked his way back up her body and hovered over her, bracing himself with his arms.

She wrapped her legs around his waist and clasped his shoulders. "A girl could get used to having you around," Dani said, her voice wavering ever so slightly and her eyes glistened.

Need. A primal, visceral ache beat a slow drum against his sternum.

He nudged his cock head between her slick folds, gave her a lopsided grin and brushed her tangled, damp hair from her brow. "You've got me for now," he said with a hint of a laugh. No point in letting her know he gave a damn. But deep down, if he was honest with himself, he'd pursue this full on if she'd truly been a PA and not a warrior.

"Do I ever." She didn't break her gaze from his, moving beneath him. "And I'm loving every minute."

His cock went deeper, buried inside her all the way to the hilt. "Not going to lie, I do too," he said, loving the awesome sensation of her tight, hot pussy enveloping him like he belonged there.

He cast a glance through the jet's small window where midnight black skies sped by. The bedroom's dim lighting illuminated his reflection. And hers. They looked like they'd always been together. And could be in the future.

"Jonah," she whispered, caressing his jaw as her eyes locked onto his in the reflection. "You feel so good... so right..."

Her heat surrounded him, flowed over his still growing cock. He plunged all the way into her until he filled her completely, sinking balls deep to the hilt.

"So do you," he said, taking her all the way to hilt again, then withdrawing only to drive into her again.

She convulsed around him. Her eyes dark as night, filled with pleasure, passion. Possession.

He closed his, blurring the ragged emotion lancing him behind his breastbone. He didn't know who had been claimed. But he didn't care. He withdrew again, then drove back into her with one long, hard stroke.

She felt right. Way too right. And yet all wrong.

BODY-TO-BODY, flesh slapping rhythmically against flesh, Danielle met every stroke, every plunge into her. Joined him in the age-old carnal dance, reaching... reaching for the release she craved. Edging closer, closer still as he filled her again and again.

He locked his mouth onto hers, drove his tongue into it, matching his penetration with each thrust, parry. Dueling with hers, bringing her to the edge. Giving her everything. Taking all of her with him.

He'd said he didn't want another woman who lived her life on the edge, yet he claimed her just the same. Made her feel more cherished than she'd ever thought possible. He'd shown her he cared without words. With his body. Tears pricked behind her eyes, Danielle told herself she didn't need... or want... to hear the words.

This. Being here. Now. Climbing together to the top had to be enough.

But for now? Tonight? Tonight the need spiraling through her, coiled tighter, sending spasms from her clit through her. She held on. Refused to let go. Afraid to fall.

He wrenched his mouth from hers. "Open your eyes," he demanded, his breath ragged. "And come with me."

The final strands of her hold on reality broke free, lashed through her. She cried his name, hanging on and convulsing around him.

"Yes," he groaned, plunging into her one last time before stiffening, his release pulsing inside her. He jerked again and again, loading the rest of his seed into her until he finally collapsed on top of her.

She could feel his heart pounding against her chest. Heard the rasping breaths he took and she held onto him, stroking the length of his smooth, muscular back. Then she held him close, not ready to let him leave her.

"Damn. God. You...," he rasped. "You make me weak."

Her pulse stuttered and tripped in her throat, filling her with emotion. A sob escaped and then she heaved a deep breath to push the rest of her long buried tears down.

"Hey," Jonah said, rising up to hover over her again. "What's wrong?"

"Sorry. I..." She looked away. How had she let this man get past her defenses? Why did he have to be the one to reach inside her? "Must be pent up adrenaline messing with my mind." Not an emotional connection she didn't dare act upon. Not if he refused to take the risk and stay.

Huge mistake to get involved during a cover op. With her partner! Not good. Not good at all. But yet...

He caressed her cheek. "You're crying," Jonah said softly. "Talk to me. Tell me what's really going on in your head."

Her mouth went dry like the desert during a windstorm. She'd never felt so raw, so exposed to another human. "This, us, wasn't supposed to happen."

"But it did and here we are."

"We'd never have gone past first base if you'd known who, what, I am all those months ago."

"I don't regret that weekend."

"Neither do I, but if I'd known they'd recruit you..."

"I volunteered," he said, cutting her off.

"Still, I'd have asked for a different man. Because I... I..." She stopped, still not understanding the instant attraction she'd experienced with Jonah. Finally, she continued, "Everything had happened so fast, I didn't have time to think things through." Though the memories of their first time together blurred with the speed, the rush of their connection.

"Look, it's okay. I wanted you. You wanted me. And you didn't want to take things slow."

No. He was like a walking male pheromone then. And now. "I bet I'm not the only woman who jumped into bed with you right away."

He laughed. "No." He kissed the top of her head. "But you're the first woman to leave me without giving me a way to reach her again."

"Because I got called back to CRUSH to take care of an emergency and you'd already told me you didn't want to date another military person," she said quietly. "For reasons I totally understand."

"Thanks. I'm sorry I hurt you though," he said, pulling the blankets over them while rolling over to hold her. "But I'm not sorry I got to see you again, especially since your neck was on the line."

"It'll be on the line again."

"I know, but if anyone can take care of herself, it's you." He brushed a tendril of her hair from her brow and kissed her forehead. "You're smart. Tough. An excellent partner in the field."

Her heart cracked a little. Oh, how she wished she could believe in the safety, the security of simply being with him. In the quiet moments of intimacy that a couple shared. And even in the scarier moments when they had to fight for their lives.

But she understood his position after what she'd been through as a teenager. Her parents' deaths had shattered her. Her uncle had been good to her. But he'd never replaced her mother and father. And when she'd buried her emotions, her tears and grief, to focus on fighting injustice and terror, he'd welcomed her facade with relief.

Then she and her uncle talked about battle ops and averting devastating wars. Her life had changed the day the suicide bomber killed her parents. She'd spend the rest of her days protecting the innocent from the machinations of evil people.

That meant exposing herself to danger and increased the likelihood of her death.

"I can't be the woman you want. We both know it." She trailed her hand over his muscular chest and over his perfect abs. So strong. So honorable. So stubbornly unattainable.

"I'm not asking you to change. I get your commitment." Jonah tightened his hold. "I have the same one."

They had so much to bind them. He wouldn't ask her to change for him, but she knew the kind of woman he desired. A safe one, not one who chased danger in the name of justice. Not permanently. She'd rather be alone than compromise her standards for any man.

But she wasn't alone tonight. Nor did she want to think about the road ahead.

"We don't have to make this into a big deal." Danielle moved her hands lower... and lower still until she reached the thatch of hair arrowing straight to his groin. Then she rolled on top of Jonah and straddled him. "However, we have a few more hours before this jet lands in Frankfurt. Why don't we make the most of them?"

He held her waist, thrust deep inside her again. "That's an excellent idea."

Jonah pulled her down to lay on him, bringing her closer... too close. Still, she loved the way he moved in her with gentle, slow strokes while caressing her with his strong, sure hands. And, as he brought her to the edge of reason once more, she loved spinning out of control with him. Together, they crested over the peak, flying into the abyss together.

When he brought her back, holding her and loving her with his mouth, his hands. And when she heard his whispered words of endearment, she lost herself to them, wishing only for a moment in the possibilities they presented. But happily ever after didn't exist except in fairy tales and romance novels.

CHAPTER 6

"WE'VE BEEN HERE THREE DAYS," Dani said as she looked through her telescope at the conference center. Her uncle would give his acceptance speech for the World Philanthropist Award on Saturday and he refused to back down. "No sign of the terrorists we lost track of back in Afghanistan. Damn it. I want to know how they evaporated when our satellites should have been trained on them."

Jonah tucked his shirt into his designer pants. Something had shifted between them during their flight over to Frankfurt. But when Esther had informed them about the missing terrorists after they'd checked into the five-star hotel, Dani refused to mix pleasure with business.

He didn't blame her. And agreed that they needed to focus on catching the potential assassin and his partners. But tamping down his attraction had been a hell of a distraction.

"You told me someone on the inside of your agency betrayed you." He lifted his jacket, shrugged it on and then walked to where she stood. "Could that same person be responsible for the satellite's malfunction?"

She played with the emerald teardrop pendant on her platinum gold chain. Fake, but high quality. No one could tell the difference unless they had a jeweler's eyepiece on. "Perhaps. But that could be anyone and we don't have time to figure out who or what caused the satellite's failure." Dani smoothed her hand down her silver couture dress, which cinched in at her slender waist and flowed over her full hips in a stream of chiffon and sparkling beads. "Hopefully, the Russian can give us a fresh lead."

She turned from him and the gown gaped at the back, revealing her bare skin. Lust careened hot blood straight into his dick. It throbbed, hardened as an erotic slide show flashed through his brain. He couldn't get the memories of their night in the private jet out of his randy head. "Uh… you forgot to zip all the way up," he said hoarsely, willing his hard on to fucking take a hike.

She stopped in her tracks, then reached behind her. "Damn it. I meant to ask for help, but…"

"Here. Let me." He didn't wait, tugging the zipper

to hide the delectable skin he'd tasted plenty of times only days earlier. He withdrew his hand, but not before tingles zoomed through his fingers where he'd touched her. *Get back to business before you forget why you're here in the first place.* "Dimitri won't do more than continue surveillance on the three properties where El Muhunnad might be holed up." He stepped back, then caught sight of her mismatched shoes.

So much for *focus.* Neither of them were shooting with both cylinders.

"Dani," he said. "You sure you're okay with your decision to keep me out of your bed?"

"What are you talking about? Of course I am. Why wouldn't I be?"

He smiled, then pointed to her feet.

She flushed and huffed a breath. "Simple mistake."

"If you say so," he said, unable to hide the laugh in his voice.

She held his eyes for an instant and electricity crackled between them. "I do," she said, breaking her gaze before stomping off to the bedroom.

Dani returned a few minutes later with matching shoes. Ignoring him, she moved to the credenza near the small foyer and picked up her clutch. "Dimitri will be at the gala tonight," she said without breaking her stride.

They'd hooked up with the elusive Russian at a local cafe. He'd given them intel about El Muhunnad's potential locations. The man had been matter-of-fact, all business. And didn't promise them more than surveillance of the properties.

But he'd arranged to attend tonight's gala for reasons still a mystery to Jonah.

"Dimitri will be there," he reminded her again. "So might the people who want to kill your uncle."

"That's why we're going," Dani said, pausing by the closet to open the safe.

She withdrew a thigh high holster with a pistol from it. Both items, along with his concealed gun, had been developed for smuggling through metal detectors. It didn't escape him that if they had the ability to get through security without detection, their enemies could too.

She moved the slit of her sexy gown and fastened the holster to her upper thigh. "Dimitri wants to stop them as much as we do based on my agency's recent intelligence about his operations."

Jonah's mouth went dry. More heat shot to his groin again, making his designer pants uncomfortably tight. He cleared his throat and averted his gaze to the pair of gold embossed invitations on the coffee table. They'd procured invitations through her agency's connections to the gala where several dignitaries would be in attendance. Most hailed from the European Union.

"We should go." He picked them up and tucked

them into his shirt's breast pocket. "Your uncle clear about our instructions?"

"He's staying in tonight due to a slight cold," Dani said. "Not that he's happy about my being here. But as long as we're not seen together, no one should make the connection."

"There'll be a lot of people there. Someone might recognize you." Not him. He'd never been to an event of this magnitude.

"I only care about two of them."

A Saudi prince and oil magnate, Kasim Riyad, with deep pockets, and an American socialite who had recently acquired a high-tech company in the United States. One that had shady deals with multiple known criminal organizations throughout the world.

The dark web had provided more intel about the players Jonah and Danielle would shadow tonight.

Jonah stepped over to Danielle, closing the scant distance between them. "You're sure no one will link you to Abarron?"

"My disguised eye and hair color will help. That and the fact I haven't been photographed with my uncle since I turned eighteen will keep our enemies off my tail. Plus, you don't look a thing like the man they thought played on their side when you infiltrated their terrorist cell."

"This one's good." He played with a lock of the blonde-haired wig she'd put on before they'd deplaned. "You're gorgeous as a green-eyed blonde, but I prefer brunettes." Especially this one.

The pulse in the base of her throat fluttered wildly. "Flattery will get you nowhere." She covered her exposed, vulnerable neck with her hand and rubbed the telltale reaction to him as if trying to wipe him out of her mind.

"Point taken," he said, then twirled the hair once more before releasing it. But he might just return to teasing a little more out of Danielle before this mission ended.

"Ready Mrs. Martin?" he asked, then picked up her wrap and draped it over her shoulders, lingering long enough to feel the heat shimmering on her skin when he lightly touched her.

"Absolutely."

She moved away from him toward the suite's door, but he heard the waver in her voice, caught the slight hitch in her breath and his blood roared in his ears. Not being with him had been crazy bad for her too.

He caught up to her. "You realize you can't give me the cold shoulder once we're out in public?" he asked as he opened the door to the penthouse room's hallway.

"Isn't that what married couples do?" she asked as they made their way to the elevator. "And don't worry. I can play my part quite well, thank you."

Hell. He'd been unsettled for days by the craving,

the desire, the need hollowing him out. They'd started something on the flight over and now he couldn't stop his hunger. No one else had ever had this kind of effect on him. But could he give up his SEAL career and join forces with her permanently? Even knowing something, someone could take her away from him at any moment?

But no meant no even when the woman denying them both what they desperately wanted was lying to herself… to him…

"If you say so." He pushed the button to call the elevator to their floor, then placed his hand on the small of her back, ready for their charade. "But that doesn't explain why you almost walked out of our suite wearing two different shoes."

JONAH'S HAND branded her skin. And the humor in his voice nearly undid Danielle's resolve to maintain a professional distance after they'd arrived in Frankfurt. She liked him. He had a steady presence and an easy sense of humor. She'd always been so serious and Jonah brought out something in her she'd deliberately tapped down until he'd freed it again.

But she didn't dare allow him to crawl under her skin farther than he had already crept into.

The elevator dinged and the gleaming metal

doors opened. "I made a simple mistake with my shoe mix-up," Danielle said. "Changes nothing." *Liar.* Oh. How in the hell could she get through this operation without touching him… being with him… having him until she had to let him go?

"Sure thing," he said easily, guiding her inside. "But anytime you want to revisit your decision to keep your hands off me, let me know."

Desire swirled a hot trail through her, firing in her belly, breasts, and between her legs. She shouldn't, couldn't, let this heat determine her actions. But she still wanted him despite his unwillingness to be with a woman who constantly put herself in harm's way. He liked her, but he couldn't accept her profession. Her back still turned to the closing doors, she stared at the mirrored wall in front of her, and weighed her options. Right now, she could act on every lusty thought blazing through her veins and into all of her erogenous zones. As Jonah's fake wife…

"Well," she said carefully as she pushed the Lobby floor button. "We can do anything we want while we're masquerading as a married couple. I suggest we make the most of the time we have whenever we're not chasing potential terrorists. At least that way we can pay more attention to the task at hand instead of avoiding each other day and night."

"What's the catch?"

"We're getting this out of our system once and for all, but no more cozy post-sex confessions or cuddling all night long in bed." Not when he had no intention to stick around.

"Just good old-fashioned sex?" He roamed his hands from her waist to the underside of her breasts. "No strings attached?" He reached around her and the elevator stopped moving.

"Yes."

"You drive a tough bargain," he whispered, caressing her nipples through the dress's fabric. "I'll agree on one condition."

The tips hardened into buds, lanced wicked arrows of need straight to her sex. Her legs trembled, weakening with every tweak and stroke. Right now she'd do anything to have him continue touching every inch of her body.

"Name it," she moaned, her thong panties damp with her hot, wet and demanding arousal.

He moved one hand to the slit of her dress and slid it inside, stroked the tender flesh of her inner thighs. "We keep in touch and check in with each other now and then. After the mission's over."

She ached, the exquisite tugging sensation in her throbbing clit had her clinging to the edge of reason, struggling to think straight. "Why's that so important to you?"

"I happen to like you, Dani. Is that so hard to believe?"

"I…" She liked him too. Way too much. She didn't know if she could pretend she didn't want more than that from him but… oh, she didn't know if she could deny the need pinging along her nerves, begging for his touch.

He pushed his finger beneath her silk thong, then teased the seam of her wet folds. "Well?" he asked, stroking his fingers over her clit. "Do we have a deal?"

Her heart beat faster, pulsing in tandem with the pressure building at her core, coiling tighter, tighter still. "What if someone figures out what we're doing in here?" she half-moaned, not sure she cared who caught them in the act.

"Maybe they will." He pushed a finger into her and she nearly jumped out of her Jimmy Choo heels. "Maybe they won't. So. Do we have a deal?"

He pressed his groin into her butt, then moved his erection over her bare ass with small circular motions. Mimicking everything she wanted him to do to her. She ground against his cock, the friction of the fabric adding heat to her arousal.

Crazy. So fucking crazy she didn't recognize herself in the elevator's mirrored walls.

She wanted to be that woman—sexy, desired, craved by a man so incredibly masculine and powerful… him. "God. Yes…," Danielle gasped. Only Jonah could make her throw caution to the curb with a stiletto inspired high kick.

"Excellent."

"Do it now. Fast. I can't…" she moaned, every inch of her fully attuned to the need firing in all her senses.

"God. You're so damn hot. I can't wait to bury my cock into you again." He drove his finger in and out of her, faster, deeper… "Come Dani. Let yourself go."

Excitement, ecstasy. Exquisite throbbing pleasure raced through her body, building pressure. Coiling tighter, pulsing hot. "Jonah…," she moaned, reaching for her release.

He rammed his finger into her again, put another on her clit, flicking the bundle of nerves. "That's it. Give yourself to me. All of you," he commanded.

Closing her eyes, she clung to him, arching her back to thrust her breast into his other hand. And her orgasm whipped through her, hurtling her over the precipice, stars bursting until she slowly landed back into herself.

Dimly, she heard his last words echoing in her brain, but they floated away like soap bubbles rising until they snapped, popped… pinged.

"Just turned off the emergency hold," Jonah said quietly.

The elevator moved again as he spoke. Reality knocked her into her senses again. She snapped her eyes open and they broke away from each other. "We're almost there," she said, straightening her dress's skirt and throwing a healthy mental dose of nails pounding into coffins to annihilate the last remnants of her desire.

But still wishing the elevator had never begun descending to the ground floor.

CHAPTER 7

"HOLD ON," Jonah said, withdrawing his pocket handkerchief from his suit's breast pocket.

"Hurry." Danielle pressed the 'door closed' button on the panel when it reached the lobby.

Jonah cleaned up the evidence of their naughty encounter, then neatly tucked it into his back pocket. "Let's do this," he said.

Releasing the button, she waited for the doors to slide open. How could she have let him... how could she not?

Jonah took her by the elbow, jarring her out of her thoughts, then escorted her out into the hotel's lobby.

Adrenaline spiked along her nerves as she caught sight of their contact, Dimitri-No-Last-Name, in the distance observing them.

Casual. Brooding. Seemingly unaware of his

surroundings. But as the doors opened, he discretely pointed toward a hotel server person walking into the main lobby.

Danielle's pulse ratcheted up a notch, but she kept her breathing even despite the thundering in her ears. She immediately recognized the man despite his disguise as he continued moving through the hotel. But then she'd recognize her would-be rapist/murderer's slight hitch in his hip's gait anywhere. He'd walked around her on the ground after they had captured her, kicking her torso, legs and arms as she shielded her head from the blows.

She and Jonah looked nothing like the time the bastard had captured her. Still, though she knew their new disguises would protect them, her heart tattooed the inside of her ribcage.

Air drained from her lungs. She dragged in a shaky breath as the clickety-click of her heels on the polished marble floor clanged inside her brain. An unwanted wave of dizziness brought black spots into her vision.

Her knees wobbled, and she moved into Jonah's steadying grip. "El Muhunnad's got someone on the Grandhotel's payroll," she murmured, resuming her regular stride, no longer panicked, determined to keep the bastard in her line of sight.

"You can't let him know you've made him," Jonah said, forcing her to slow down.

Aggravation. Disappointment. Pent up anger fired

into her temples. "What if we lose him again?" she asked through gritted, fake smiling teeth.

"He's not going anywhere." Jonah guided her toward their Russian contact who had begun to stroll toward the ballroom's entrance. "Not until he hooks up with the rest of his team."

They easily made their way through security, then cruised into the ballroom. Walking side-by-side, they strolled through an opulent blend of traditional cream colored marble, an arcade of arched columns topped by scrolling Corinthian capitals where modern, linen covered high tables dotted the floor. Vases filled with greenery, white roses and pale pink tipped peonies filled the air with a sweet, floral scent.

People who'd arrived before Danielle and Jonah milled throughout the vast interior, plucking canapés from banquet tables and the servers weaving throughout the space. Soft pop music piped through hidden speakers and a clear space for dancing with a huge, disco ball hanging from the ceiling overhead. Chattering, the sound of cutlery clinking and champagne corks popping gave the room a festive feeling.

But behind the veil of opulence and luxury slept an angry vipers' nest of people who would do anything in their power to destroy western civiliza-tion... in the name of morality, but Danielle knew the truth. Greed undergirded their lofty motivation.

And in the process, they'd take down the good

and peaceful people in their countries too. No one was safe. Ever.

They approached Dimitri who sipped from a tumbler filled with ice and a clear liquid. "Ah, Jack, Diane," he said enthusiastically. "How long has it been since we last saw each other?"

Jonah smiled easily. "Too long."

"Dimitri, how are you?" Danielle asked while continuing to survey the crowd milling around the room with their cocktails in hand.

"Fine. As always." He kissed Danielle on both cheeks, whispering a quick warning, then held her at arms' length. "Jack. You'll have to keep an extra eye on your gorgeous wife tonight. I might just steal her from you."

Danielle listened to Jonah's response with ice permeating every inch of her soul. Their exchange had been brief, but she'd heard everything she needed to know before he'd released her.

Evidence that the terrorists had developed sophisticated bombs disguised as smart phones. They'd easily get smuggled into the conference center. If they didn't find and disarm all the weapons, more innocent victims would die. She'd coordinate with the CRUSH agents in the vicinity to make sure that didn't happen. And they'd have to find the person responsible for creating the technology after neutralizing this threat.

"Oh, Dimitri, you're such a flatterer." Danielle

linked her arm into Jonah's and gave her fake husband a 100 percent, full on look of adoration worthy of an Oscar. "But you know Jack's the only man for me."

"*Da*." He nodded. "An unfortunate fact for me, but I suppose I can live with it if you save me a dance later."

Code for meeting him to go over the counter intelligence. "Of course. I'd love to," she said. "Jack, let's mingle and see if we can't drum up more contacts for Providence Technology's future business."

"I like the way you think," Jonah said. "We'll talk later, Dimitri."

"I'm sure we will," he said. "I'll touch base with your favorite person before we rendezvous on the dance floor."

"Wonderful," she said as Jonah lifted a champagne flute from a server's tray. "I'm sure she'll love hearing from you," she said as Dimitri bowed slightly, then stepped away from them. Her agency's founder had deep connections all over the world, but Danielle doubted she'd be thrilled with the latest turn of events.

Another man came into view in the opposite corner of the ballroom next to a banquet table covered with dishes filled with pastries and fruit. She recognized him immediately despite the added pounds and new hair color. Her stomach twisted, tangled into a ball of knots. Acid crawled into her throat. She forced herself to swallow it down and pressed her hand against her belly.

"We've got company," she said as Dimitri disappeared into the crowd. "Twelve o'clock, and he's not here to mingle." Even worse, he'd put a huge wrench in their plans if he figured out the blonde socialite on Jack Martin's arm was the woman who'd put him away for industrial espionage three years ago.

"How the hell did he get out?" Dani muttered, turning to face Jonah and moving closer to him.

Instant heat warred with the adrenaline popping along his nerves. "How the hell did who…" he said, scanning the room in the direction she'd been facing seconds earlier.

"Never mind who," she snapped. "Kiss me until the blond, overweight dude in the one-size-too-small tux standing next to the banquet table leaves."

He didn't like the tiny line of worry between her brows. Or the way the corpulent forty-something man casually moved from the table without filling a plate. Not when he caught the guy surreptitiously stealing furtive glances around the ballroom.

"Who is he?" he asked, closing the scant distance between him and Dani to hold her tighter. Damn. Every muscle in her body had contracted. He stroked his hands down the ramrod straight back until he reached the dip just above her full ass. "And how does he factor into what we're doing?" He brushed his lips over her ear, still studying the man as he leaned against a pillar and texted.

"Graham Miller. I caught him stealing corporate classified information from my uncle's company," she whispered a breath away from his mouth. "Used to be with the American missile program. They sent him to Israel to collaborate with Omega Operations Company about counteracting the hyper glide vehicles—missiles that dodge traditional radar systems. But I'd gotten intel from the head of CRUSH's central command he'd been recruited to steal corporate technology. Ours, specifically."

He smoothed his palm over the small indentation, and then a bit lower to the sweet spot he'd discovered the first time they'd fucked. "Could he be part of the plot to kill Abarron?"

Dani trailed small kisses along his jawline and then returned to press one against his mouth. "I'm sure he is," she said. "Graham's been locked up for three years and wasn't supposed to get released until he served another seven. I just wish I knew how he got out without our knowledge."

His stomach twisted into a knot, pulled tight. Frustration stabbed into his temples. "Who were his clients?" Jonah snapped his attention back to Graham when he flagged down a server.

She held his gaze. "How do you think I found out about El Muhunnad?"

He froze momentarily, then squeezed the bridge of his nose. "Makes sense, but that means your agency mole covered up Graham's early release."

"I agree, so he must know I'm here."

"And he'll know about our fake identities."

"We have to stop him from exposing us before it's too late."

"We've got to get him alone. Away from the crowd." There was one way to prevent Graham from blowing their cover. Go their separate ways until he neutralized the problem. "I'll shadow him while you hook up with Dimitri."

"I'll give him the details, then we'll rendezvous at the designated meeting place at twenty hundred hours."

"Sounds good." She caressed his cheek and pressed another kiss on his lips. "I'll go freshen up. Graham and whoever he's here to meet probably won't need to use those facilities and that'll give me time to radio my superiors. Tell them to investigate the source of the leak."

She had her head together and didn't miss a beat. He liked her confidence. Admired her for it. "Solid plan."

She stepped away from him. "We've got to move fast," Dani said matter-of-factly, then she swiveled and walked away before he could reply.

Trusting her to handle her end of the bargain, Jonah crossed the carpeted floor, weaving around other attendees with a slow, deliberate pace toward his target. He side-stepped another server and circled another group of guests, then reached the west side with its rows of floor to ceiling pillars.

Using them for cover, he made his way to the pillar where the man stood and approached him from behind. Discreetly, and thanking the tech gurus of her agency for their clever weapons, he withdrew his Glock and slipped it into his coat's pocket. Still holding the gun, he moved to stand next to Graham and gently pressed the barrel into the guy's pudgy torso.

"Don't move a muscle," Jonah said before the man could speak. "Not unless I give you permission."

"Who are you?"

He refused to answer Graham's question, pushing the hidden barrel deeper into the man's corpulent flesh. "Walk with me and act like you want to." Given the guy's heavy weight, Jonah figured the bastard couldn't outrun him. Nor would he risk exposing himself to security when he still had time to serve and clients to appease.

Sweat beaded on Graham's scalp line. "Of course," he mumbled. "I never say no to a better alliance."

They walked side by side toward the ballroom's entrance where Dimitri and Dani now stood. "You've played both sides of the fence too long, but I'll run it by my partner," he said, then caught up with them. "Scumbag wants to make a deal."

"No surprise there," Dani said grimly. "Graham, how did you get out without our detecting you?"

"You're not the only person in this room with interesting connections," he said. "I won't reveal mine unless you guarantee my safe passage out of Frankfurt."

"You're not in a position to negotiate." Dani tilted her head toward the exit. "Dimitri, take him and do what you have to do to make him talk."

Graham's eyes bulged and the pearls of water on his hairline tracked down his brow. "You're going to let him torture me?" he squeaked.

"I'm sure you'll talk as soon as he pulls out the electrodes."

Her voice was harsh, low and brooked no argument. Jonah never liked taking extreme measure to flip a suspect, but he'd accepted the ugly side of war just as he'd learned to mourn the deaths of his team members.

Still, he put his hand on her shoulder. "Why don't we let Dimitri's men hold him until we're through tonight. Then we can pressure him to spill," Jonah said as a woman entered the ballroom. Her slinky, red gown left nothing to the imagination. "Ashley Townsend's here. We need to make our move. Dimitri? You got someplace to stash this jerk?"

Their Russian counterpart nodded, then clapped

their prisoner on the shoulder. Immediately, Graham's eyes glazed over and he slumped against Jonah in a near dead weight.

"Seems you hit the vodka too hard, comrade," Dimitri said, he hefted their prisoner's arm under his bracing arm. "Go. Get to your target. I'll take it from here."

"Excellent." Jonah moved to stand next to Dani, coiled his arm around her waist. "We'll hook up at the same rendezvous point later tonight. And go over the bomb detection procedure before the conference tomorrow."

They parted company and Jonah saw two other men join Dimitri to help him with his load. Laughing and joking about Americans not being able to hold their top-of-the-line Russian vodka.

"Let's do this," he said, though he didn't like the quick flash of fear and worry lighting in Dani's eyes before she schooled her face into a placid, gorgeous mask.

Whatever she'd learned when she'd contacted headquarters had freaked her. But with their first suspect heading toward the ballroom's dining tables, he didn't have time to talk. He'd save that conversation for later.

CHAPTER 8

AN HOUR LATER, after attaching tracking devices to Ashley Townsend's clutch and the Saudi oil magnate's smart phone, Jonah escorted Danielle to the dance floor. Bruno Mars' *Versace on the Floor* slowed the pace down and he held her close... his clean, masculine scent once again invading her senses, making her want him all over again. But she shook off the desire. Only the mission mattered. And they had plenty of trouble to face before completing their duty.

"What's got you so freaked out?" he said softly in her ear as he stroked his palm down her back and tugged her into his body.

The band that had wrapped around her chest the minute she'd heard her commander's information squeezed tighter. Ice invaded her veins. Everything they'd worked toward saving had been jeopardized.

"Marily Kohn's our mole," she said, still reeling from the shock of the information her agency's leader had revealed.

"I thought you and she were friends."

His low voice, the breath whispering over her skin, failed to warm her. The painful knowledge she'd acquired punctuated her fragile connection with Jonah. Today she'd lost someone she'd counted on—Marily—through a terrible betrayal. In less than a week, she'd say goodbye to Jonah when he returned to his SEAL team. Sure. They'd part as friends, but they'd probably never see each other again despite Jonah's request they check in with each other in the future.

Surviving a breakup had been hard once before. But she'd gotten through the worst by focusing on her operations for CRUSH. Choosing to work for the secret agency had been the right decision even at the cost of losing her boyfriend.

But she knew deep down she'd miss Jonah so much more. Because she needed him. Needed his friendship… needed the promise of more with him.

Emotion scraped her throat raw. Old hurts, guilt and grief, arrowed into her gut. "Marily and I've been friends since we met in the Israeli Defense Force," she said unable to hide the feelings punching her in the belly. "I recruited her after she finished her mandatory tour of duty."

"I'm sorry, Dani," he said. "What's your evidence?"

He swayed with her, holding her to him with his powerful arms. She allowed herself a moment to soak in his strength and more. "She got the intel about Graham Miller's mysterious release from my commander's people in Virginia, but failed to disclose the information." Jonah's embrace tightened, and she welcomed the comfort he offered. "Plus, she's one of the few people we have who knows how to operate our reconnaissance satellites."

"She in custody now?"

"No. That's the other piece of intel that proves she's involved," Danielle said. "She vanished yesterday. No idea if she's betrayed our location or our mission." Either way, she wouldn't back down from her commitment to bring down the bastards who'd targeted her uncle.

"You want to abort?"

"Hell no. I haven't come this far to stop now. We'll assume we're in the clear until we determine otherwise. That'll give CRUSH time to get more operatives in place to continue the hunt for El Muhunnad's leader. That's our primary initiative," she said. "Saving Uncle Abarron and preventing them from bombing the conference center is part of our objective."

"We've had a ton of curve balls thrown our way. No plan ever survives first contact with the enemy," he said. "We're prepared to see this through even if the shit hits the fan."

The music changed to a faster song by Maroon 5, forcing them to break their contact. Dancing faster, she twirled around him, then leaned in closer. "We'll do what it takes even if we have to bend the rules," she said. "You still on board?"

He placed his hands on her waist and moved in tandem with her. "Comes with the territory. Not going to que…" He stopped talking and brought her into his body. "Guy who captured you in Afghanistan is making his move."

Her pulse accelerated, pinging adrenaline into her legs and arms. "Where?"

"Directly behind you. Heading to the kitchen with Ashley Townsend." He turned her, pressing her backside into his chest and groin.

"We'll let the tracking device do its job, but we've got to get out of here without drawing suspicion," she said, then swiveled to face him while creating distance between them and dancing closer to the opposite side of the dance floor.

"Dimitri's making his move." Jonah followed her, smiling and shooting her a smoldering glance, then reaching for her.

Danielle took his hand and continued dancing, leading him toward their intended targets. She touched her earring and turned on the radio communicator concealed inside. "Looks like the Saudi, Kasim Riyad, is exiting too," she said, then calmly spoke to the operative working behind the scenes.

"Our targets are on the move. We're following the suspects. Tell Dimitri we're scuttling our rendezvous."

"Could be a trap." Jonah stepped off the dance floor with her. "We've got to take this slow and easy."

"Exactly." She smiled at the passing server as they wove their way through the crowd of partiers to get closer to the front of the ballroom. "Either they're in league together or Ashley Townsend's in trouble."

"We don't want to tip our hands. Trust the tracking devices." Jonah stopped by a tall, linen-covered table where canapés and small plates had been placed, then picked up a cracker with a combi-nation of pickled fig and ricotta. "Here." He held the appetizer to her mouth. "Try this. What's your com agent got for us?"

She complied, the burst of savory and sweet dancing on her tongue. But the delicious flavor transformed to sawdust when she heard the pop of a silencer in her ear, then nothing but static.

Her heart raced, and she choked down her bite. "Jonah," she said, grabbing his arm. "We lost our communications contact." That meant they had no choice but to go on without ground support.

JONAH DIDN'T HESITATE, dropping the appetizer and pressing his palm to the small of her back. "Let's roll,"

he said, slipping his other hand into his suit jacket pocket to get his gun ready once they got out of the ballroom.

He steered her through the crowd, smiling casually and moving at a normal pace until they'd exited the gala. "Hotel room first. Change into our gear."

"Yes. I'll let command central know what's going on. But we're on our own until reinforcements arrive."

Skirting the lobby, they made their way to the bank of elevators. He punched the penthouse suite buttons for all the lifts. When the first one arrived, the doors opened to let out its passengers, then Jonah guided her inside.

Minutes later, they entered their dimly lit suite which carried a cloying scent in the air.

Cold fingers clutched his heart, squeezed out every icy beat. Someone had been in the room or still remained. Without speaking, he and Dani pulled out their guns, signaling to each other as they cased first the living room.

Once they'd ascertained the all-clear in that room, they made their way one by one, covering each other with each movement into the bedroom. The scent grew stronger and Dani mouthed Marily's name.

The aroma of iron mingled with the woman's perfume. Blood, the stench unmistakable, had been spilled here tonight.

His muscles tensed and every hair on the back of

his neck stood at attention. Nothing good waited for them behind the closed bathroom door.

Carefully, he tilted his head toward it. Dani slipped stealthily in that direction, cradling her gun, then leaned against the wall next to the door's hinges. Jonah followed until he reached the opposite wall.

She flicked her fingers... one, then two and on her mark three... he pushed the handle down, rapidly pushing the door open. Gun first, he swung into the space.

Marily lay sprawled next to the toilet, moaning. A knife wound penetrated her exposed stomach. "You're too late." She coughed and pink spittle foamed on her mouth. "Nothing will stop El Muhunnad now."

Dani moved around him, then knelt next to the prone woman. "You fought beside me. Cried over our lost friends. I don't understand." She shot Jonah a direct stare, her eyes filling with tears. "Why? Who did this to you?"

Jonah jerked a towel off the rod and dropped to the marble floor. "She won't make it," he said quietly, running his hands over Marily's body. "Given her current state, I'm certain the terrorists tipped the dagger with tetrodotoxin. It's a fast acting poison. El Muhunnad's preferred way to punish traitors."

"But she betrayed us."

Blood stained her couture gown and her voice

carried more than grief... outrage and disbelief tinged her words.

"They thought I set them up after you escaped...," Marily hacked harder and more pink tinged foam tracked down her cheeks, "and captured me... brought me here to make an example out of me for you to find... for you to learn what'll happen when they catch you again."

Adrenaline reverberated through his nerves, exploded in his temples with lightning speed. Dani's life would always be in danger no matter what she did for a living. "Damn it, El Muhunnad's put a bounty on your head, Dani."

"I figured they would once they discovered my identity," she said without missing a beat. "Don't worry about it. I can handle myself."

Her matter-of-fact response echoed off the blood-covered bathroom tiles. He digested her words, came to the sickening conclusion that he'd lose her one day to violence. Marily cut into his thoughts, hacking as she spit out more foam and venom.

"You're lucky he saved you, but your luck will run out eventually," she said, coughing and twisting away from Jonah.

"Why did you betray your country... your people?" she demanded.

"Your fucking uncle betrayed my father when he falsely accused him of industrial espionage... he died in jail at the end of a bedsheet," Marily hissed, cutting her off as she spasmed. "Die bitch." She twisted again, and in a flash jerked out a gun, fired at Dani.

Dani swerved out of the bullet's way, but not before it grazed her left arm. "It's okay. I'm good," she yelled.

"Fuck. You won't get another shot." Jonah wrestled the weapon away from Marily, her eyes dilating as the seizure intensified. "You're a dead woman now."

"I died the day my father hung himself..." She jerked one last time, then went rigid as the poison finished her off.

"You got a clean up crew for this shit?" he asked without missing a beat. "Cause we can't fuck around with the authorities on this one."

"Yes." She pressed her palm over her grazed arm. "I'll alert them now."

He winced when she smeared the blood onto her dress. "You need medics?" He doubted she'd stop to get treatment of any kind, but he had to ask. He had to know if she'd accept other people's help when she needed it most.

"No, this wound doesn't require stitches."

Determination underpinned her answer. Told him exactly what he'd expected to hear. Though he respected her dedication, he couldn't bring himself to see her die for her cause. That had been tough enough once before. And what he'd felt for Sandy paled compared to how much he'd grown to care about Dani.

"Excellent, then we can get on with stopping El Muhunnad before they kill thousands of people who haven't got a clue about the danger they're in." He didn't include her uncle in his assertion. Now he wanted to get in, do the job, and get out before he made a complete fool of himself and revealed his feelings.

Dani needed no one to care about her. She figured out how to do it on her own.

"We'll head back to the living room," she said. "And get changed. Going to be a long ass night."

"Agreed." He stood, then stripped off his jacket and shirt while striding out of the bathroom without waiting for her. They had an op to complete, and then he had a life to reclaim.

And that life wouldn't include her. Nope. He didn't want to worry every second of every day if he'd be a widower. He'd head back to his unit, finish out his tour, and move on.

DANIELLE'S THROAT CONSTRICTED, scraped raw. Jonah wouldn't, couldn't, accept her choices. And yet, he made similar ones every day. While she understood his reasoning—his trying to avoid the pain of losing another person he loved—she'd hoped he'd see beyond his stubborn desire to control reality and realize he had more to lose by walking away from her.

But he didn't. And so she had to let him go.

She shook her head, willed the tears pricking behind her eyes to go away. Marily's attempt to kill her had failed, but her former friend could be right. Danielle's luck could run out one day. But not today. And not until she understood what had really happened all those years ago.

"I never knew you, did I?" she asked the dead woman she'd fought side by side with for years while wiping her hands down her bloodstained dress.

Quickly, she dressed her wound without casting the woman she'd once called friend another look, and made her way into the suite's living room.

Jonah had changed into black tactical pants, slipped on his special ops multi-mode headgear and cold weather fleece jacket. Loading their firearms and black ops equipment into a backpack, he said, "Warn your uncle about the security breach. Get him under cover ASAP." He tucked another round of ammunition into the bag.

His voice was calm, cool, collected and detached.

She tugged the top of her zipper from behind, jerking it low until she could pull the damn thing down and stepped out of the gown without modesty. The only thing that mattered was stopping a murder and countless other deaths.

"I refuse to let El Muhunnad's schemes succeed," she said, just as coolly while walking to the bedroom's closet. She grabbed her own gear, then changed rapidly while continuing to speak. "Marily Kohn clearly was delusional. I've been with my uncle since the terrorists murdered my parents. There has to be another explanation for what happened to her father. Either way, I don't have time to investigate her accusations. Not now."

"True." He tossed her a second pack. "Load your gear," he said. "We won't be returning to this suite."

While she'd lost the chance for more with Jonah, she still kept his loyalty and she valued his partnership in the field. "The agency will arrange new accommodations for us," she said, adding her own bungee cords, clips, and firearm into her bag with quiet efficiency.

Hoisting it onto her back, she moved out of the bedroom, exchanged her fancy earring radio for a standard issue communicator. "Send in a cleanup crew, then transfer Abarron to the safe house on the outskirts of Frankfurt," she commanded as she stepped into the hallway.

The response she heard had her nerves firing a thousand rounds of electrical charges, each one making her insides quiver. "My uncle's missing," she said to Jonah, pushing to go faster. "His entire security team is dead."

"We'll find him," Jonah said without missing a beat.

"We might be too late." Danielle couldn't figure out why the terrorists would move ahead of schedule unless they had ulterior motives besides just murdering her uncle. "They'll torture him. Try to get all his intel about the new technology he's developing to counter the hyper glide vehicle missiles."

"Checking our target suspects' locations now." Jonah withdrew his GPS tracking tablet and scanned the screen. "Two are still in the hotel. One is en route to the Frankfurt airport."

Her heartbeat slowed to a dull beat. If they didn't stop the terrorists before they took her uncle out of the country, they'd never find him again. Let alone find him alive. "My bet is on the one heading to the airport."

"We'll eliminate the first two before we assume anything."

"But…"

"You know I'm right. We take this step by step or we're sure to lose him."

"What floor?" she asked as they made their way to the service elevator next to the dimly lit concierge lounge, the skeletal outlines of empty tables and chairs a stark contrast to the party they'd attended.

"Fifteenth."

Using a special pass keycard, they accessed the lift and rode it down, then they raced to the room where they'd detected both suspects. "I'll go in last," Jonah said. "Cover you."

Using the same keycard, he unlocked the door with a click, then showed his count to go inside. They burst into the room, her ahead of him so both could scan the room with their guns ready to shoot only to find the socialite and the Saudi Oil Magnate fucking each other senseless, their moans filling the air.

"What the fuck?" Ashley Townsend yelled, scrambling to push her lover off her.

Danielle ignored the socialite's outrage, leveled her gun at them. "What have you done with Abarron Ginsberg?"

"Who?" she asked.

"I'm not buying your innocent act. You're involved in his kidnapping."

Kasim reached for the bedside drawer and she pulled the trigger, the silencer popping softly as her bullet pinged next to the man's hand.

He recoiled, held his hands up in surrender. "We know nothing about your uncle."

Oh, he knew more than he let on, but she didn't want to waste her energy interrogating either of them. "You're lying," she said as Jonah made his way into the bathroom.

"All clear," he called.

She tapped her ear piece. "Send in reinforcements to Room 1506. You'll find a package waiting for you in there." Danielle didn't hesitate, knowing she couldn't stay here to guard the pair, but refusing to let them go. "Tie them up. I'll let the rest of my team deal with them. I'm sure they'll talk once they're given a shot of sodium Pentothal."

"I'll sue. You can't do this," Ashley screamed.

Checking the drawer, she spotted the gun and withdrew it, then she tucked it into her back waist-band. "Gag her first." Danielle didn't betray the emotion pounding against her sternum. Her uncle had been her lifeboat during the worst days of her life. If she lost him too... She held them at gunpoint while Jonah gagged their suspects, then used plastic ties to secure them, hands behind their backs and feet bound to the hotel's desk legs.

"They won't be going anywhere now," he said when he finished.

"If they get him out of Frankfurt..." Her trigger finger itched, adrenaline surging through her body as they made their way back to the room's door.

Jonah grabbed the Do Not Disturb sign and hung it on the room's handle. "We'll beat them there."

"We have to," she said, breaking into a run... not sure if she was running to save her uncle or trying to outrun the overwhelming loneliness that had haunted her throughout her life.

Minutes later, Jonah zipped their vehicle through the streets of Frankfurt toward the airport at least twenty minutes from the city's center. Danielle continued sending reports to her superiors and the dozens of agents scattered throughout the city.

"Shouldn't be long now," Jonah said, entering the autobahn and accelerating to max speed.

She gripped the worry handle, relayed another report to Dimitri, then told Jonah. "No movement at their hideout," she said.

"Bomb squad on the scene?" he asked, maneuvering around a line of trucks.

"Yes. And the conference officials cancelled my uncle's speech." She hoped his life wasn't in the balance too.

Jonah hadn't wavered in the aftermath of the events leading to this moment. He'd stayed true to accomplishing their objectives. A dull ache settled low, then anchored a boulder over her chest making every breath she took a huge undertaking. Yes. She still had a great team player fighting with her, but she'd lost the man she'd grown to care for far too much.

CHAPTER 9

"LOCATION OF TARGET IS LOGIHUB, a logistics technology warehouse with an airstrip for its private jets," Dani said coolly as Jonah exited the autobahn.

"In or out of airport security limits?" He made his way to the place Dani had indicated with a pointed finger on the GPS map.

"Outside," she said after a tense beat of silence. "We'll want backup, but we don't want to alert the suspects." She spoke into her earpiece. "Is everyone in place? Good. Hold your positions until I signal you."

"How many people do we have at our disposal?" he asked.

"Six. They're highly trained operatives who'll do whatever it takes to rescue my uncle at my command." She pointed to the overhead sign. "Exit here."

Complying, he drove onto a road next to the main

thoroughfare which led to the bustling hotel city where travelers making connections stayed overnight. Soon, instead of bright lights in windows along with rail cars zooming to and from the terminals, they were driving through the darkness on a two-lane road leading to their objective.

"Infrared goggles." She pulled two pair out of the bags they'd packed earlier. "Headlights off."

He put his on with one hand, then adjusted his vision to the eerie glow of the moonlight illuminating the vineyards plump with grapes ripening for the year's autumn harvest. Windfarm mills revolved in the shadows, their modern sleek lines a stark contrast to the country's old world villages with their centuries old castles and churches.

"Target is moving," Dani said without a trace of emotion in her voice. "What's our ETA?"

"Five minutes tops." Jonah accelerated toward the building coming into view in the distance. "We'll ditch the SUV when we get closer."

"Great. Any idea how many terrorists we're up against?" Jonah asked. They were two lone agents, one of them related to the kidnap victim. While she'd remained detached since they'd discovered Marily, he couldn't be sure for how long. And he sure as hell wasn't sure if he could remain detached if another bullet came close to killing her.

But he had to keep his brain in the game and focus on rescuing the man who had given Dani a home after the suicide bomber killed her parents. Otherwise, he'd blow the mission.

"Pull in here," she said, pointing to a narrow, dirt road just ahead with twin lines of beech trees on either side of it.

He swerved onto the farm road, then eased the SUV over to the left, parking next to the gnarled trunks. Wordlessly, they exited the vehicle with their gear. After applying black slashes of grease paint onto their cheeks and pulling their caps low, they armed themselves.

Making their way through the rows of vines, they alternated their positions to the front, covering each other with perfect precision as they made their way toward the warehouse. Wind rustled through the leaves, carried the scents of rich, fertile earth and the sweet smelling grapes ripening for harvest.

Twenty feet from the warehouse's front side, Jonah raised his hand and motioned for her to stand next to him. "We've got to move fast to save your uncle," he said, scoping the private airway tarmac on the opposite side of the three-story building.

Two man wearing tactical black gear and balaclavas to cover their faces patrolled the backside of the building armed with Russian AK-12 rifles. They crossed at the center, paused and laughter echoed off the white-washed cement walls. "Rooftop's got two more armed men, most likely another pair are patrolling the front hangar doors," Jonah said.

"We'll take the men on the ground out first, then use their radio coms to ascertain how many others are waiting inside."

Though the temperature had become chilly, Jonah's internal heat levels increased and his muscles tightened in readiness. At his signal, they dropped to the ground, then crawled forward on their bellies. "We go in slow and easy," he said while they edged closer. "Then find your uncle."

Shouts in Dari. Orders to load their cargo and secure the warehouse echoed.

"Yes," Dani said, pushing closer to the last row of vines between them and the enemy agents.

Spotting a mechanical grape harvester within five feet, Jonah pointed to it. "This way," he said.

Once again, they moved together as if they'd always been a tactical team. Damn. He liked it. He liked her. Hell, he liked everything they did together, even as they made their way toward danger.

They stood, Dani facing back and he the front, then with their weapons ready to fire, they cut across the ancient roots and dirt until they reached the harvester. Peering around the tall, red engine compartment, he watched the first two guards light cigarettes. Overhead the men on the rooftop held their positions forward and aft.

Dani tracked his lines of vision and then met his eyes with hers. Grim determination swam in their depths, and she silently moved into position behind him. With an imperceptible nudge, she gave the signal to act before the men guarding the back parted to walk to their posts again.

With speed, and a stealth born out of years of training, they breached the distance until they reached the guards. Death came with swift snaps of their necks long before the men could react to their presence.

After relieving the guards of their walkie talkies, they made their way to the western edge of the building with their backs against the exterior wall.

"Two down," Jonah said, glancing around the corner. "Clear."

"Six to go," she said while they rounded the corner and made their way to the next corner.

He moved around it, snapped the next guard's neck without hesitation. Beside him, Dani fired several rounds and took out three more men before their enemies' bullets could stop them from reaching their objective.

Taking out one of the rooftop guards, he ran toward the huge opening with a private jet exiting the building. The sound of the engine overpowering the voices of the men shouting orders in Dari.

"Cargo is loaded," he yelled. "We've got to stop the plane before they takeoff."

He rushed another man, taking him out with a bullet while she raced toward the jet, shooting the wheels. They popped, and the jet stalled, bumping to a halt on the jagged, fractured tires.

A black helicopter with her agency's coat of arms on the side panel whirled into view. It hovered overhead; the blades whirling. The copter engine's whine mingled with the jet's. A flurry of wind kicked loose leaves and twigs, sending them into the air. They swirled viciously around the compound as two people dressed in black rappelled down ropes, shooting the remaining terrorist on the rooftop along with three more on the ground.

They jumped to the ground, then shot the enemy while Jonah raced to the plane, tossing a rope with a hook onto the wing. He pulled himself onto it and grappled with the fuselage's door. Busting into the cabin, he heard fire power. A shot blazed by his head, but he grabbed the first man to attack him. And wrestled him to the ground.

"Give me the cockpit's entry code or die now," he demanded in Dari.

The man shook his head. "No code. You're the one who'll die today."

No code meant no way in unless... the retina, facial recognition technology flashed. "Not if I have anything to say about it," Jonah said roughly, then snapped the bastard's neck while more bullets pinged inside the cabin.

Using the terrorist's body as a shield, he walked backward into the food entryway, then pushed the man's face into the pad just outside the cockpit, prying the dead man's eyes open. The door unlocked, and he shoved the man off him while forcing his way inside.

Jonah popped the pilot in the head with a bullet. The copilot screamed, steering to the left and speeding up at the same time on rickety, broken wheels which screeched violently. He shot the man, but he couldn't stop the careening jet, which swerved violently, the fuselage crashing to the ground.

Before he could brace himself, he lifted into the air, hitting the roof.

Stars burst behind his eyes and pain shot through his skull, bringing him to his knees next to the instrument panel. "Fuck," he yelled, scrambling toward the open cockpit door. As he approached the main cabin, Abarron's prone body slumped over in his tilted seat while the man who'd captured Dani days earlier worked to loosen his seatbelt, a steel blade glinting just above its scabbard.

The acrid scent of jet fuel wafted into the interior. One wrong move and the entire thing would blow.

Which would suck because he still wanted another chance with Dani. He had to get out of this in one piece so he could prove they deserved one more shot to get things right between them. He didn't want a homemaker and safe, uncomplicated woman. He wanted a warrior and a fighter and a passionate woman. He wanted her.

DANIELLE KILLED ONE MORE GUARD, continued shooting at the enemy to give Jonah cover and enough time to reach the jet. Wind, the chopper's blades whirling tat-a-tat-tats, the sound of gunfire all around her didn't distract her from her ultimate goal.

Save Abarron at all costs.

Running toward the jet, every sound amplified and ricocheted through her body as it sped up, screeching on the tarmac until it careened to the side and slithered into the vines. "Take cover," Danielle yelled, stopping in her tracks and dropping to the ground.

She raised her forearm to her head to block the debris of splintered wood and metal shards from hitting her. Sweat tracked down her face and into her eyes, stinging them. Swiping them, she smelled the fumes of jet fuel before she registered the fluid draining from the tanks.

Her heart punched against her sternum, but the blood it pumped ran like sludge through her veins. Panic, fear. Dread clawed the inside of her throat. *Get a grip. Uncle Abbaron is in there... Jonah's in there too... Jonah.* Now she understood his fears, the reasons he fought his desire to be with her in the ways that counted. The same terror roared through her, catapulted from her chest and slammed into her ribcage.

Her agency's helicopter's pilot radioed. "Asking

for another chopper to bring fire extinguishing equipment and bambi buckets to douse a potential fire."

She caught the horror filling her mind, lassoed it into submission and transformed the adrenaline into action. No way would she let either man die tonight. "I can't wait for it to arrive," Danielle said, coming to her feet and then sprinting toward the jet. "El Muhunnad will murder them if I don't stop them."

Her heart pounding in her throat, she closed the last remaining yards between her and the fuselage. After removing her rappel rope from her hip holder, she tossed the grappling hook over the edge of the open cabin door. Pulling herself up, she ignored the radioed orders and barked commands to the people surrounding her outside, focusing on getting inside.

Carefully, she positioned herself over the edge. Relief coursed through her, and her muscles slackened their wound up tension when Jonah appeared below. Alive. Thank God he was still alive.

Quickly, she lowered herself to where he'd crawled. "Are you okay? Any injuries?" she asked softly when she reached his side and glanced at the back of the passenger cabin where her uncle hung from his seat, unconscious.

"Just bumps and bruises. Nothing worse." He tilted his head toward the rows of toppled seats. "We've got to save Abarron and get the hell out of here before the fucking jet blows."

She tracked his gaze. The terrorist who'd captured her days earlier struggled to get out of his seatbelt two rows in front of her uncle. "Shit. If he frees himself before we get to Abarron…" already she could see the jerk gyrating to get loose, desperately reaching for his dagger.

"Go to your uncle," Jonah said. "I'll neutralize the bastard before he does."

"Don't get killed."

"You either," he said, then kissed her swiftly.

What happened next would depend a lot on both of them. But the quick brush of his mouth over hers bubbled through her like fine champagne.

"Let's do this."

Using the tilted chair armrest as footholds, she and Jonah pushed their way toward her uncle, still unconscious, before the nameless terrorist freed himself. Every muscle in her body coiled with tension, and adrenaline raced through her nerves, making them zing.

The terrorist slipped out of his seat and tumbled to the opposite side of the aisle. Tasting metal, her pulse skipping in her throat, she reached for the bastard's leg before he toppled onto Jonah.

"Dani, look out," Jonah called, then launched himself on top of the man, breaking her grip. "He's got a dagger. Save your uncle, I've got this."

"Uncle Abarron, wake up," she yelled, desperate to warn him. "Please, don't give up now. Come back." He'd fight for his life if he regained consciousness.

She grasped the armrest across from her, her feet unsteady on the chair back, knowing she'd have to choose between one man or the other. But Danielle had lived a half-life for too long.

"I love you, Jonah," Danielle called.

"I love you right back." Jonah rolled to the portal window, taking the terrorist round and round with him. "I'm going to spend every day making you believe we're perfect for each other."

Something in her heart shifted. He sounded like the man she'd grown to rely on in every way. "Same here." She refused to give up now when she had everything she'd ever wanted and didn't even know she needed within her grasp.

The terrorist continued to wage war with Jonah, but her guy had the upper hand, gripping the bastard in a choke hold. And the dagger's steel glinted through the strap on the leg she'd just gripped.

Adrenaline careened into every pore and her pulse sped up to autobahn speeds. "Keep pinning him," she yelled as she crawled over the seats toward them and then she clasped the terrorists ankle.

The jerk struggled, kicked out, landing a blow on her shoulder, then another on her face. She held on until she wrapped her hand around the blade's handle and jerked the deadly dagger from its leg scabbard.

"This is for the innocent," she yelled, stabbing his leg with what she now knew had poison on the tip based on Marily's death.

A blood-curdling scream filled the interior, and he jerked, kicking once more, the desperate last flails of a dying man.

The blow landed to the side of her head. Pain ricocheted through her temples and black dots danced in front her eyes. Her vision blurred. For a moment, she couldn't see, couldn't hear... then Jonah's voice reverberated inside her head and she regained her focus.

His gleaming blue eyes held hers. "You scared the living shit out of me," he said, cradling her face with his big, strong hands. "Thought I'd never get a chance to do this again." He brushed his mouth against hers before pulling away. "Now let's get your uncle out of here so we can get started with doing more of the same for the rest of our lives."

Heat radiated through her and bubbled in her veins like effervescent champagne had just been popped in her heart. "Does this mean you'll reconsider my job offer and join CRUSH?" she asked.

"Affirmative."

He kissed her again, and she welcomed him, loving the sensation of his mouth on hers and loving how he'd completed her in ways she'd never dreamed possible.

EPILOGUE

DECEMBER

"YOU TOTALLY SURPRISED YOUR PARENTS," Dani said, snuggling into Jonah's arms while the logs in the fireplace in front of her flickered and glowed.

She traced a finger over the princess cut diamond ring Jonah had given her when he'd proposed nine months earlier. Her wedding band had joined the glittering jewel a month later during a private ceremony at a winery in Israel.

Jonah chuckled and covered her hand with his. "I think they're going to want us to pop out another grandchild now that everyone in my family is expecting."

"Ha. Not going to happen soon," she said as the fire crackled, snapped, sending bright yellow sparks into the flue. "We've got to get back to headquarters and get our agents out in the field. El Muhunnad's leader is still out there." Though they'd prevented a catastrophe over a year ago, the terrorists' top commander remained at large.

"We've got a worldwide organization hunting for the bastard." Jonah drew her closer, kissed the top of her head. "He or she can't remain underground forever."

"Too bad Marily scuttled all her intel before she died."

"Yeah. And she'd betrayed you for a grudge that had no ground in reality," he said. "Your uncle tried to save her father from ruin, but his mental illness fed all his delusions."

She tilted her head to take in Jonah's handsome face. Firelight danced over the planes of his cheeks, one with a thin scar underlining the right side's bone. The one he'd gotten the day he rescued her from the terrorist compound. His piercing blue eyes reflected the flames, rimming his black pupils with bold color.

He'd chosen to join her agency. Still fighting for justice, but able to navigate around the bureaucracy.

"Do you miss the states?" she asked. "I mean we could always… move and live closer to your family." His parents, brothers and sister along with their spouses had welcomed her with open arms. Much love, laughter, life had echoed in the living room earlier today.

Though she'd enjoyed every moment today while celebrating their traditional Christmas, she treasured this quiet midnight moment in their bedroom suite where they had already lit the third candle in her Hanukkah menorah.

He caressed her cheek. "I dig CRUSH's headquarters in Israel," he said. "Plus, I adore the commanding officer who oversees the operations."

"And I adore my new second-in-command," she said, still marveling at how much her life had changed. Over a year ago, she'd been alone, not realizing how much, fighting but never stopping long enough to let someone in… to love. Now she had Jonah who stood by her… her partner and friend, her lover and husband.

"Maybe when we do decide to have children, we can split our time between America and Israel," she said. "After all, I am a dual citizen." Her parents had her while they'd lived in New York, then two years later they'd claimed their Israeli citizenship.

"Sure. That could work, but not for a few more years," Jonah said, tilting her chin up and lowering his head to brush his lips across hers. "I want you all to myself."

"Same." Though for the first time in her life, she no longer feared becoming a mother one day. Plus, the excitement about the current batch of children coming into the world had kick-started her biological clock. "I don't think either of us is ready to get out of the field."

"Damn straight."

"Good," she said, coiling her hands around his neck to bring his mouth to hers. "I love you."

"I love you right back," he said, then kissed her, holding her close, parting her lips with his tongue.

She welcomed it, tangling hers against his, loving the sensations building inside her body. Loving him even more tonight than when she'd first spoken the words to him. Here, in his arms, she'd found a true partner, an equal. They'd promised each other a lifetime together. One she claimed every hour, every day, and every night. Because with Jonah, she believed in all the possibilities... all the hopes and dreams... and in all the love binding them.

I HOPE you loved Jonah and Dani's story. This Brotherhood Protectors' crossover romance is part of my sexy, action packed contemporary romance series! Covert Rescuers' Undercover Shield (C.R.U.SH./CRUSH) is an elite team of operatives acting to bring justice to the world.

CRUSH... where Courage Defies Danger and love is always on the line!

Start reading your next book CRUSH today!

. . .

INSERT COVERT SEDUCTION LINKS HERE.

IF YOU LOVE SEXY, hot contemporary romances, then jump into my Hollywood Heartbreakers' series and dive into a luscious Italian love story. Order TEMPTING THE HEARTBREAKER now!!

And to find out about new books, sign up for my newsletter!

Christine's Newsletter
Subscribers are automatically be entered for a chance to win a $25 Amazon Gift Card every month!

IF YOU LOVE action adventure romantic suspense stories with lots of HEAT, then check out my first official C.R.U.SH. (Covert Rescuers' Undercover Shield) romance COVERT SEDUCTION. It'll be available March 31st! Go ahead and PREORDER your copy today!

IF YOU LOVE contemporary romances with exotic settings, you'll love the sensual, hot and exciting romance set in a fantasy kingdom featuring Prince Santiago a la hottie and his virgin bride, Ilsa who isn't afraid to ask for sexy lessons in the bedroom! Order WRONG PRINCE, RIGHT LOVER now!

IF YOU ADORE READING contemporary romances with sexy billionaire alpha heroes, then you'll love THE MARRIAGE ULTIMATUM. This standalone romance has it all: a secret baby, revenge, an ill-fated reunion, and a marriage of convenience between two people who might want to deny their attraction but their sexual chemistry ignites and that leads to all kinds of complications and intrigue! Order THE MARRIAGE ULTIMATUM now!

IF YOU LOVE SPORTS' romances with a twist, you'll adore reading a sexy, exciting romance set in the regatta yacht racing world. Marco Delgado is out for revenge and his target is his enemy's daughter. When he proposes a Marriage of Convenience to this sexy mathematician who is a total geek, she can't say no or he'll destroy her family's shipping company. Order THE TYCOON'S RED HOT MARRIAGE MERGER now!

FOR MORE INFORMATION about all my books, including, the Brotherhood Protectors and all my standalone romances head on over to my website and check them out!

www.christineglover.com

Join my Facebook Street Team, CHRISTINE'S CRUSHES, for exclusive giveaways and sneak peeks of future books. I really appreciate your help in spreading the word FALLING FOR HER RESCUER, including telling a friend. Reviews help readers find books!

Keep reading for an excerpt from Delaney and Ethan's Brotherhood Protector's story, FALLING FOR HER BODYGUARD today!

For the first time in weeks, Delaney Lawson had plans that didn't include dodging the paparazzi or stopping to pose for pictures with her fans. Her grueling schedule during her last movie set in Montana had come to a close, but renovations at her home in Los Angeles had stalled, making it impossible to return. No biggie. When she'd accepted the role, she'd been excited to return to her home state to film the thriller. She'd been looking for an excuse to spend time in her hometown to hang out with her girl-friends and get some serious R&R. Now she had one.

Smiling, she continued driving toward Eagle Rock with her windows down, the music turned up and adding her seriously bad vocals to the lyrics.

"Sugar," she sang at the top of her lungs. "You're sweet . . ." Soon she'd be back with her friends, drinking longnecks, and dancing to jukebox Top 40 Hits at the Blue Moose Tavern.

"Honestly, please stop. You're so tone deaf you're killing the song."

She sent a sidelong glance at her friend and personal assistant Kerry Ann and grinned. "You'll survive."

"Not with my hearing intact."

"Good thing it won't be long before we reach your place, then I'll run over to the Blue Moose Tavern," she said. "I can't wait to see everyone again."

"Thanks for giving me a lift home first."

"No problem, but I wish you'd come with me. I'm sure everyone would love to catch up with you too."

"Not my gang. Besides, you know me, I'd rather sip a Cosmo at my favorite club in LA than hang around here."

"I understand." The joint didn't have much in the way of class, and Delaney had hung out in far glitzier places since moving to Los Angeles, but nothing could dampen her excitement about spending time with her friends. "Are you sure you still want to stay at your folks' place?" Delaney asked, worried Kerry Ann would feel lonely and sad in her childhood home since her parents had passed away.

"It's mine now, remember."

Delaney shook her head. "I still can't believe they're gone."

"Me, either. Dad went so fast, I barely had time to say goodbye."

"I'm sorry, Kerry Ann."

"Thanks. But I'm fine, really. Just trying to decide whether to sell the ranch or not."

"Tough decision," Delaney said, approaching another S curve.

Beside her, she caught sight of Kerry Ann gripping the Jeep's handlebar. "Still hate driving in these mountains, don't you?"

"With a burning passion of my soul."

Delaney laughed. Her best friend had a wreck the first week after getting her driver's license. "We're fine," she said, then lifted her foot from the gas pedal, and gently pressed the brake.

The Jeep continued gaining speed. Her heart thudded against her sternum. "Shit."

"What's wrong? Why aren't you slowing down?"

Fear laced Kerry Ann's voice adding fuel to Delaney's racing pulse. Her fingertips prickled. "Nothing." She hoped. She pressed the brake harder. No dice.

"This isn't funny."

The wind whipping through Delaney's hair suddenly chilled her to her bones. "Hold on," she said. "I've got this." She controlled the Jeep and steered through the S curve, keeping her hands steady on the wheel though her insides shook. Another mile and she'd approach a steeper downgrade on the road.

"We're going to crash."

"Not if I can help it," Delaney said, holding the steering wheel with one hand while pulling the emergency brake's lever. "Hold on." Nothing changed.

"I really don't want to die here."

Acid coated Delaney's tongue, and she tasted metal. Neither did she. "That's not happening. Not today." She hadn't come this far in her life to lose everything now to faulty brakes.

"Then do something."

"I will. I am." Good thing her older brothers and her dad had taught her every trick in the book when it came to navigating emergency situations. Still, her muscles quivered and everything in her body tensed. "Trust me."

Quickly, she shifted into second gear, then coasted across the dividing line to the opposite side of the highway toward the gravel shoulder. Her tires crunched over the gravel, fear skittered down her spine, but she held tight even as the Jeep fishtailed. *Please let this work. Please. Please. Please.* The world around her seemed to stand still, everything a picture-perfect shot while she slid into the beargrass and elk sledge shrubs buttressing the shoulder's edge. She turned into the skid, then crashed into an immature stand of ponderosa pines.

She heard a loud pop. Dust and the harsh slap of fabric hit her face, pushing her back against her seat. "Holy shit," she cried, the pain in her cheeks burning hot. Dazed, she shook her head and pushed away from the deployed airbag. "Are you okay?"

Kerry Ann coughed and sputtered. "I'm fine."

"Thank God."

A strong, acrid scent filled the interior and her heart thudded fast against her sternum. Up until this moment, she'd been concentrating on steering out of a potential accident. Now reality hit.

She'd crashed. Shivering, she shifted the Jeep into park, turned off the engine, and unsnapped her seatbelt which had locked her in place. "Told you we'd get out of this in one piece," she said. Still, everything ached, her skin burned, and the early evening fall temperatures were dropping steadily.

"Let's hope we're close enough for cell phone reception."

Montana's Crazy Mountains were notoriously awful for losing signals, the towers spread thin and unreliable for making calls, even during emergencies. "No kidding."

Kerry Ann reached for her purse and pulled out her phone. "We're in luck," she said. "Two bars." She showed Delaney her screen then quickly called the local service station in Eagle Rock.

"How long until the tow truck gets here?" Delaney

asked when Kerry Ann finished giving their location over the phone.

"Half an hour tops. This is one of those times I'm grateful there isn't a lot of action around here."

"Ditto." Gingerly, she gave herself a physical once over. Nothing broken. Nothing sprained. But a major bruise was already blooming at her collarbone where the seatbelt ran. Then she glanced in the rearview mirror and grimaced. "My beautician would have a conniption fit if she saw this. A bright red stripe slashed across her face. She looked at Kerry Ann who had suffered a similar, albeit less marked, fate.

"No big deal. It's not like your glam looks matter here."

"Nope. Never did." Even now, she never really believed the celebrity photos of her splashing across the headlines in the tabloids. Deep down, she'd never left behind the country girl who'd left her hometown to head to Los Angeles to chase her dreams.

"We should get out of here, wait by the side of the road to flag the tow truck down."

"I'd like to text Allie too." Her girlfriend had arranged the get-together tonight so Delaney could meet her husband Axel Swenson, a bodyguard for the Brotherhood Protectors. "I need to let her know we'll be late." She opened her door and stepped outside.

Kerry Ann joined her and they made their way through the underbrush toward the highway's shoulder. "I wish I'd worn something warmer," she said, tugging her thin sweater around her waist.

"Yeah, me too, but we'll be out of here soon enough."

"At least you remembered to trade in your stilettos for cowboy boots," Kerry Ann said ruefully. "But still. It could have been a lot worse."

"Exactly," Delaney said, texting Allie about their accident. After reassuring her that she and Kerry Ann hadn't suffered any major injuries other than a few bruises and a slight airbag rash, she accepted her friend's offer to pick them up. The sooner the better.

"Man, it's creepy out here."

Gravel bounced across the empty highway, echoing in tandem with the sound of the cool mountain breeze rustling through the trees. Branches creaked. A snap sounded. The hairs on her neck raised, and Delaney scanned the highway for the tow truck. "No kidding," she said, hoping Allie showed up soon.

Another branch cracked and Kerry Ann clutched her arm. "What's that?"

"Probably just a deer or something," she said calmly to reassure her friend, though her heart raced. Wolves had been known to roam these mountains and, with more civilization encroaching, animals were getting bolder.

"You sure?"

She looked at her Jeep, furtively searching for

anything lurking in the darkening forest. Nothing stood out despite the growing trepidation beating hard against her breastbone. "Yes," she said. But deep down, the growing blackness had her counting every second that they stood by the road waiting for help.

What had happened was probably a freak accident. And her parents just had her Jeep serviced a month ago before they went on vacation. But something didn't add up, and that made the looming night sky more ominous than ever.

ETHAN WALKER SAT across from his new boss, the scarred desk separating them. "Appreciate the opportunity to work for your company," he said.

"You came highly recommended." Hank Patterson tilted his head toward the man flanking his left side. "Swede says you were one of the best in the field. Purple Hearts aren't awarded to just anyone."

"Thanks." But the medal meant nothing compared to wishing he could get back to Afghanistan. Sure, he'd managed to protect a few of the guys in his unit by throwing himself in the line of fire, but he didn't save them all. And he'd bought himself a one-way ticket out of the Marines with his hip injury. "You have an assignment for me?" Better to focus on what he could do. Brotherhood Protectors gave him a fresh start, albeit not one he'd ever have considered before his hip had been shot through.

"Not yet, but that'll give you time to settle in first."

"You sure you don't want to bunk with me?" Swede asked, then pulled out his cell phone to glance at the screen.

Ethan shook his head. "Nah," he said. At thirty years old, he was too damn old to bunk with anyone. Besides, sharing living quarters always reminded him of his lousy childhood and the numerous foster homes he'd endured. He liked Swede. If not for him, Ethan's job prospects would have been nil to maybe a shit desk job after his medical discharge from the Marines. But being a third wheel in a newlywed's house held no appeal for Ethan.

He glanced at Swede who had a frown on his usually amiable face. "You okay?" he asked.

"Something's up with Allie," Swede said. "She was supposed to meet Delaney Lawson at Blue Moose Tavern, but they're coming here instead."

Adrenaline spiked along Ethan's nerves. "Delaney Lawson? The movie star?" Even he recognized the name—who wouldn't when she'd just won an Oscar? Plus, plenty of guys in his unit had her pictures hanging in their barracks.

"Yes. Allie said her friend just had a wreck. Monty's Service station is bringing her Jeep in, but according to Monty, things look suspicious."

Hank straightened. "Why does he think that?"

"Brakes failed." A muscle jumped in Swede's jaw. "Looks like they were deliberately tampered with according to Allie. She says they'll be here shortly."

"Looks like you might have your first assignment after all," Hank said, standing and locking eyes with Ethan.

"Come on," Swede said. "Let's not keep them waiting."

Whoa. After all Ethan had been through in Afghanistan and Iraq, who knew he'd end up protecting some Hollywood starlet against her diehard fans in the middle of nowhere. But a job was a job. "Sounds good to me."

Ethan joined his friend and Hank, pain lancing deep in his hip, but he ignored it. The damn gunshot in Afghanistan had fucked up his military career, but he wouldn't let the injury stop him from moving on.

This might not be the battlefield, but for the first time since Ethan had left rehab in Bethesda, he had a purpose: completing his first assignment at the Brotherhood Protectors and moving on with his life. If he clung to any mission, he'd forget about the last one—even if the throbbing pain in his left hip made the task almost impossible.

"Look, I don't care what you say," a shrill voice said as the ranch house's foyer filled with women, two of whom looked like they'd been through a chalk storm. "I refuse to let you go home alone when there might be someone out there trying to hurt you."

"Relax, Kerry Ann."

Ethan looked at Delaney Lawson as she tried to calm the other woman down. She was even more beautiful in person.

"I'm sure Monty's overreacting," Delaney continued.

"We could have been killed."

Swede's wife put a hand on both the women's shoulders. "You were very lucky," she said. "I agree with Kerry Ann. You need protection. My brother's team is the best in the business. I'm sure he'll . . ."

"He'll make sure you won't even know you've got a bodyguard, Delaney," Swede said, cutting in.

"But this is Eagle Rock," she protested. "My hometown has got to be the safest place in the world."

"Not always. Just ask Sadie," Hank said, then gestured toward the back of the ranch house. "Come in. We'll discuss what needs to be done in the kitchen. I'm sure Sadie will want to join us."

Kerry Ann stalked off first in her very high heels. "Excellent idea. I could use a drink after what just happened. Come on Little Miss Unafraid, and listen to the man."

"Okay." Delaney tunneled her fingers through her tangled auburn hair. "But only because I'm humoring all of you."

"Good," Hank said, nodding toward Ethan. "I've already assigned Ethan Walker to protect you."

She shot a glance toward Ethan, colored ever so

slightly, then nodded. "Naturally, I'll pay top dollar for his services."

"We'll work out the terms of the contract before you leave," Hank said. "Rest assured, he won't let you out of his sight until the authorities apprehend the culprit."

"Hopefully, that'll be sooner than later," she said, then sashayed around Ethan.

He caught a whiff of her sexy scent mingling with the after-effects of the airbag explosion. She had a natural sway that her cowboy boots enhanced— cowboy boots? Never expected a big star like her to be so down to earth—and he couldn't tear his gaze away from her, wondering about the person behind the public image.

He'd thought he'd be babysitting a spoiled movie star, not a sexy and feisty woman who ticked all the boxes in his I-want-to-do-you column when Hank gave him his assignment. Fuck. He couldn't think of her that way. Not when he'd been hired to protect her.

Still, by the time they'd all sat around Hank's kitchen table, joined by his pretty wife, Sadie, Ethan couldn't take his mind off Delaney's wide, generous mouth—full-lipped and inviting.

"How soon before we hear from Monty?" Ethan asked to get his brain back on track.

"No later than tomorrow," Hank said.

"But I don't want her alone until then," Kerry Ann

said, then took a healthy swallow of white wine. "We can't risk it."

"As I said before, Ethan won't let her out of his sight."

Delaney slanted a look his way. "I suppose so, but I really don't . . ."

"If Monty's right, you need a bodyguard," Hank said. "Ethan's a former Marine. A war decorated hero. You'll be in excellent hands with him."

"You're right. I thought something was off when the stupid brakes failed, but I keep hoping it was a mistake during the Jeep's last service. Is that so wrong?"

For the first time, Ethan heard fear in her voice. Not much. She'd modulated it well, but he'd heard it just the same. Many people would have missed the subtle undertones of dread, but he'd been trained to listen for nuances, to catch changes in body language that expressed anger, fear, and danger. "Never assume anything," he said. "You never know who wants to hurt you—even the people you think you can trust might be dangerous. Anyone else besides your parents know you're here?"

"My agent—Laurence Hunter. I told him to contact me here while my house in LA is getting renovated. He's negotiating a contract for me to act in another Trevor Maguire film. I trust Laurence as much as I trust everyone in this room," she said, standing and locking her gaze onto his.

Her green eyes knocked the breath out of his lungs. Damn. No wonder the woman was an A-List movie star. Even with her hair a mess, along with the fine dust of white powder coating her hair, her figure-hugging jeans and her practical denim jacket she was, in a word, gorgeous.

Jeez. Get a fucking grip. Of course, she's gorgeous. But I'm here to do a job that doesn't include screwing her. "Then we'll leave it to Hank and the Brotherhood Protectors, along with the authorities to find the person responsible for your accident," Ethan said. "The only person I'm concerned about is you."

He'd treat this job like any other mission. Get in. Do what was expected of him. Protect his hot Hollywood star, then move on to the next client.

DISCOVER WHAT HAPPENS NEXT and order FALLING FOR HER BODYGUARD now!

bringing back my sexy red hot heroes, Blake Johnston AKA Quinn Sawyer, Zach Tanner, and Caleb Gibson. Be on the look out for these sizzling stories in 2020!

Red Hot Fling

Red Hot Reunion

Red Hot Proposal

and as a special bonus... Red Hot Holiday!

Be the first to hear about my new releases.

One random newsletter subscriber will be chosen every month to receive a $25 Gift Card! Sign up today by clicking on the link below!

Christine's Newsletter

ACKNOWLEDGMENTS

Many thanks to my incredible critique partners, Pam Mantovani and Carmen Falcone. You always give you incredible feedback and I love working with you! You make me a better writer with your honesty and support!

A huge thank you to my wonderful Beta Reader, Heidi Scribner. You're questions and comments made me go even deeper into making this story shine! I truly can't imagine being on this journey without you, my first reader.

As always, thank you to Elle James for creating this fabulous Brotherhood Protectors' World! Your generosity and guidance are inspirational!

Big shout out to all my other readers! You're the reason I sit in my chair for hours, alone in a room to write these love stories. This journey is all the sweeter because of you!

Major appreciation goes to my fabulous family and friends. They keep me sane, bring me chocolate and wine, and joy!! Lots of joy. Keep pouring and I'll keep on writing!!

ABOUT CHRISTINE GLOVER

USA Today Bestselling Author Christine Glover writes sexy, intriguing contemporary romances. She loves discovering how her determined heroines and super sexy heroes with heart journey toward their own happily ever afters. Her characters are real people from all walks of life who embody classic love stories with a modern twist. She enjoys finding the silly in the serious, making wine out of sour grapes, and giving people giggle fits along with heartfelt hugs. When she's not writing, you can find her traveling the world, cooking gourmet food, and desperately seeking a corkscrew.

If you enjoyed this book and would like to leave an honest review, Christine would really appreciate it because that's how other readers discover their new Happily Ever Afters.

Hang Out with Christine

Sign Up for Christine's Newsletter
Follow Christine on BookBub

Join Christine's Crushes

www.christineglover.com
christinegloverauthor@gmail.com

BROTHERHOOD PROTECTORS

ORIGINAL SERIES BY ELLE JAMES

ABOUT ELLE JAMES

ELLE JAMES also writing as MYLA JACKSON is a *New York Times* and *USA Today* Bestselling author of books including cowboys, intrigues and paranormal adventures that keep her readers on the edges of their seats. With over eighty works in a variety of sub-genres and lengths she has published with Harlequin, Samhain, Ellora's Cave, Kensington, Cleis Press, and Avon. When she's not at her computer, she's traveling, snow skiing, boating, or riding her ATV, dreaming up new stories. Learn more about Elle James at www.ellejames.com

Website | Facebook | Twitter | GoodReads | Newsletter | BookBub | Amazon

Follow Elle!
www.ellejames.com
ellejames@ellejames.com

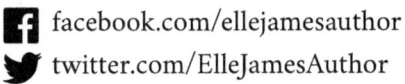

facebook.com/ellejamesauthor
twitter.com/ElleJamesAuthor